MIND TRAP

By

Barbara Ann Derksen

Hi Gina
Don't loose sleep
while reading this
book - but enjoy
Barb.

ISBN: 1-4107-2211-2 (e-book)
ISBN: 1-4107-2212-0 (Paperback)

This book is printed on acid free paper.

1stBooks – rev. 04/03/03

ACKNOWLEGMENTS

I wish to thank the Lord for giving me the gift of writing and then providing me with the wherewithal to become a published writer. I wish to also thank several people who have added their support and skills to the completion of this book. Without the support of my husband, Neil, this book would not have ever been started. I have appreciated the time he took to proof each and every page. I also wish to thank Linda Blackwood who took many hours out of her busy schedule to edit Mind Trap, Melanie Miller for providing the preface, and my friends for their words of encouragement as I sat by my computer for hours putting this story on paper.

PREFACE

There is a direct correlation between childhood abuse and adult anger manifestation. An innate freedom of choice is given to each person. We are created in the image of God, with this ability to choose. When deprived of that ability the axis of life is tilted, setting a possible stage for our un-doing. The degree of restriction or humbling, personalities and environment, dictate a response that cannot necessarily be predicted.

In the abuse of children, there is a malevolent expression towards innocence. The violence is experienced towards the physical body, yet the real damage is done in the soul area; the mind, will and emotions. The affect of the abuse is double edged. One side deprives the child of free choice by disallowing a proper reaction towards the attacker. The child is then faced with fear and a secret beyond his or her escape. The other side is being subject to maturing emotions, possibly recognizing the violation, and being unable to remedy or change the incident.

Another heinous dynamic is the seed concept. A child has experienced an act of violence. Though not of his or her choosing, seeds have been planted in the soul area. Depending on life's environment these seeds will produce in some fashion. Some people are driven to extreme in education, sports, career, etc. There is perfectionism striven for which robs them of a peace and satisfaction. It has all the outside appearance of health yet the underlying motivation comes from the humbling of abuse.

While there are a variety of other examples to site, the manifestation of anger to the point of violence is the subject of this novel. There is really nothing "novel" concerning this behavior followed years after childhood violence. To be defiled and humbled during the early years could be compared to a top with a spring wind-up. The top is wound by pushing the spring down. Perhaps a small amount of spinning occurs but it is again pressed down lest control be lost. The attacker fears the loss of control and may maintain contact in order to intimidate the victim or at the time of the original assault (s), thoughts of intimidation were planted. Either way the intent is to suppress, and depress so that truth would not be revealed. At some point, for a variety of reasons, the victim, like the top, spins without restraint and either conscientiously or uncontrolled, leaves a path of destruction resultant from its unwinding.

Choice is one of the greatest, most powerful gifts given to mankind. There are great consequences to a life when there is violation and depravation of this gift. Unequaled is this offense to mankind. The Words of Christ would seem to uphold this contention. *"But if anyone causes one of these little ones who trusts in me to lose faith, it would be better for that person to be thrown into the sea with a large millstone tied around the neck. How terrible it will be for anyone who causes others to sin. Temptation to do wrong is inevitable, but how terrible it will be for the person who does the tempting." Matthew 18:6-7 NLT*

Melanie Miller, BBC, M. Div.

CHAPTER ONE

"Debra, if you don't learn to control your temper, our marriage is over," hollered Jerry Wiebe. "I can't take much more of these outbursts and neither can the kids."

"That's just fine. Leave then and take them with you," Debra shouted right back as she grabbed her coat from the front hall closet and stormed out the door. Jerry quickly followed her down the four steps to the concrete pathway leading to the driveway.

"Where do you think you're going," he yelled.

"As far away from you and this place as I can get." Her eyes were blazing when she looked at him. Jerry felt as if she hated him and everyone in their home. As she turned on the ignition for the second time, the grinding noise was loud enough for the neighbors to hear. Debra yanked on the gearshift to put the car in reverse and then backed out of the driveway.

"You're in no condition to drive, Debra. Get back here and we'll figure this out," he shouted but Debra had already backed the car onto the street. She floored the gas pedal and spun the tires as she squealed all the way through the nearest intersection and out of sight.

She had never felt so furious. The anger burned in her head and made her face hurt. She wanted to throw something or hit somebody. Although they were living on their own now, word of their sons' activities still controlled their life. The final straw that threw her into a fit beyond control was when she had heard the news that one of them had been picked up by the police for drunken driving. Would they never grow up? When would they learn that they were headed for a life of nothing but trouble. Oh-h-h-h, she could scream.

Her whitened knuckles gripped the steering wheel as she traveled over the bridge towards the center of town. What a way to begin her day, she thought. The thought seemed to come from another person, however. This morning was one of those times when her children talked as little as possible to her and everyone joked about her needing her morning coffee. What did they know anyway? She had every right to be angry. Look at what that son of hers had done to her again. The pounding in her head was making it difficult to concentrate on her driving.

The morning was sunny. "Too bright," she groused as she put her sunglasses on. At only nine o'clock, the traffic was already thinning out as she angrily made her way toward the interstate. "I'm getting as far away from them as I can," she shouted inside the empty car. The rage felt like a ball or rock inside her trying to choke her. Her head felt as if it was stuffed with something other than her brain, like she was under the control of a thing growing inside her. Anger seemed to blaze from her eyes making them white hot and burn with the need for release.

All of the drivers around her seemed to be doing anything they could to make her angrier and their indifference to what they were doing wrong, caused her to rage all the more.

"Look out, you pickle brain," she yelled to a driver that had just cut her off. THEY'RE always talking about women drivers and yet THEY are just as bad if not worse, she thought.

"Where did you get your license?" She swerved. Narrowly missing another driver, who changed lanes without looking, she spilled one of the bottles of perfume she carried in the back seat. "That damn stuff better not

3

make a mess in my car," she ground out between clenched teeth as a smell erupted in clouds of odiferous chemicals. Her uncontrollable rage was making her the one who was driving erratically although at that moment in time she would not have admitted that to anyone. She had one delivery to make this morning and then she could leave town. Maybe she could find a little out of the way motel and hide away from all the demands her life had become.

The night before had seemed so short. Of course, those teenagers of hers continued to be the cause of her nighttime worries. When they were living at home, she used to lie awake listening for them, worrying about whom they would try to sneak in or whether or not they were doing drugs. Now, the worry was what she didn't know was happening but her imagination concocted anyway.

"How could we have raised such overly selfish, self-centered kids?" she boiled inside. "They just want to live off their parents, have their kind of fun, with no thought given to the younger members of the family or the influence they exert over them." Her rage grew even deeper as her mind went over the last four years. "They think the whole world revolves around them and them alone."

Her staying home to raise them had meant nothing. Her becoming a believer in Jesus Christ hadn't helped anything and had certainly not kept them out of the satanic realm. She hated her children for the turmoil they had been causing. The quiet restful home she had tried to create was a shambles. Arguments, anger, tears, distrust, nightly inquisitions, interrupted sleep, and many other unhealthy traits described the way their once tranquil surroundings had become since the boys began acting out.

"Watch out, you idiot," she yelled again at a car that had just turned into her lane in front of her. "Are all the nuts out driving this morning?"

Debra continued her dismal analysis of the place she called home. Since their two oldest boys had moved out on their own a few months ago, she had been spared the intrusion of night time visitors sneaking through the basement windows, girls urinating under her bedroom window and the police ringing the doorbell at all hours. But she worried, nonetheless, about how they were eating or whether or not they still had their jobs. She knew that the crowd they hung with were into drugs, a fact that was constantly at the forefront of any thought she had about their living conditions.

She worried about the choices they were making that would scar them for life. However, she and her husband seemed unable to stop their downward slide. The boys didn't care. As long as their life wasn't meddled with, they were happy or so they said.

The rock of anger inside her was intense, getting larger as she began to experience an almost blinding rage Glancing off to the right, she spotted a young man who was waiting at a bus stop. His baggy, unkempt appearance made her think again of the disreputable crowd her sons had embraced. "There, look at that long-haired punk. Probably just another kid rebelling against all known authority in his life with no care given to the people he hurts. The world, and certainly his family, would be better off without him," she muttered to herself.

Unconsciously, she felt her large, almost vintage Pontiac veering towards the young man standing next to the bus shack. Unaware of any danger, he glanced up just as the big boat of a car went over the roadside curb toward him. His face reflected his terror as his brain quickly calculated what was about to happen. A mournful scream echoed through the streets when his body was slammed against the stone wall and like a limp rag, bones broke when the weight of the big car pinned him to the wall. The ball of pain in her head grew larger so she backed up and, amidst his screams of pain, hit him again with as much force as she could gain in so short a distance.

Not comprehending what she had just done, and concentrating instead on the ball of pain that was in her head, she seemed oblivious to the screams of the bystanders as she threw her car into reverse for a few feet. To the horror of everyone watching, she once again lurched the car forward toward the bloody heap of flesh that lay in an unconscious pile at the base of the wall.

The sickening crunch of his breaking bones was audible even inside the car. Blood was everywhere, mixed with unrecognizable lumps of flesh from the body. Oblivious to the horrific events that had just transpired, Debra was aware of nothing but the rage and the anger and the pain inside her head. She wanted to break everything in sight. She wanted to throw rocks through windows, punch people in their faces, bite people, but above all smash down this wall. All sense of reason had, for the time being, left her.

With her car now immobilized, Debra was forced to sit still. She could feel her gasping search for breath come at a slower pace and her heart rate drop. Her eyes darted around at the terrified faces surrounding her car. Her pulse slowly accelerated again when her mind began to comprehend the fear and the excitement that was palpable from the people scurrying around outside. Her anger gave way to confusion. Why were people looking at her the way they were?

She rolled down her window to ask what had happened. One man, a rather large person, carefully approached the car and reached through to the steering wheel. He grabbed hold of it and yanked it from her hands, unsure of what he was trying to accomplish, but knowing that she had to be stopped. Debra immediately started to feel defensive. She could feel this man's obvious fear but couldn't understand why.

To everyone's relief, a young beat cop, Constable Jacobs, appeared within minutes. Having heard all the noise and the terrified screams from the young man, he still couldn't believe what he saw. Since trying to gather relevant information from the bystanders, all who were shouting and talking at the same time, was a wasted effort, he immediately radioed the Communication Center on his hand held radio. Located at the police station, the personnel at the Communication Center would send an ambulance.

He could see that something was under the car so he forced himself to approach it to see if the person could possibly still be alive. His stomach lurched when he bent down and saw what was left of the young man, and he quickly turned away to keep from losing his recently eaten breakfast. Even an untrained eye could see that there was no life left in what was once a son or a brother. The man was dead, that was for sure.

Debra was staring straight ahead when he approached on the driver's side. He asked, "What happened here?" but she seemed not to know what he was talking about. Assuming that she was also injured, he requested that she stay put but he took her keys out of the ignition. It was as if she wasn't paying attention to anything or anyone. In fact she appeared to be at peace if that was possible.

While waiting for the paramedics to arrive, Jacobs approached two people talking in a heated manner by the bus shack. They both began speaking at once and were able to make it very clear that the woman seemed to have deliberately run into this man twice and had been about to ram him a third time when one of them had foolishly taken hold of the steering wheel just as the car died. She had murdered the man in cold blood.

When the ambulance arrived on the scene, the paramedics confirmed that the man under the car was dead so Jacobs phoned the Com Center once again, this time to ask them to contact the county attorney. He requested a search warrant for body fluids which he planned to serve to Debra and he also requested that the county attorney be present since he now knew this was a murder scene. The nearest Department of Criminal Investigation team was also notified.

Jacobs returned to the car. Debra looked at him with glazed eyes as he reached inside the car for her purse. "Whatever your story is, lady, you're going to get lots of opportunity to tell it", he told her as he cuffed her to the steering wheel of the car. Inside her purse he found her identification.

The woman's pacifism worried him. She just seemed to be dead inside and limp on the outside. His curiosity was certainly aroused since she didn't look the type to deliberately murder someone and yet he knew what he was seeing. As he looked under the car he saw the remains, for the pile of bloody flesh and broken bones couldn't really be called a body anymore.

He straightened up and looked at her. "What happened here?" he asked her again as she continued to stare at her hands. "I don't know," she answered in a voice so quiet he had to lean in the window to hear her. Just then the paramedics arrived and quickly approached the car to examine her.

"You may have whiplash and some broken ribs, M'am," they said. "We will want you to come to the hospital for some x-rays."

"She can go but not until an officer can go with her," stated Jacobs as a squad car pulled up. The county attorney emerged from the back seat along with the county coroner. Two patrolmen were seated in the front seat.

"Can one of you escort this lady to the hospital?" Jacobs asked.

"Here is your search warrant," interjected Tom Dyer from the county attorney's office.

"Take this with you," Jacobs told the officer who planned to escort Debra in the ambulance. "We'll want blood tests and urine tests for blood alcohol levels and drugs."

As Debra was removed gently from the car she said, "One minute I'm driving along, the next I'm sitting in the car with my hands cuffed to the wheel. Why did you do that?" She didn't raise her voice at all but just asked her question in that quiet, stunned sort of voice. The paramedics moved her towards the waiting ambulance but she looked back at Constable Jacobs hoping for an answer to all the questions running through her mind.

Jacobs was a large man with a certain amount of compassion. However, there was so much evidence that it was a deliberate act that he had trouble feeling anything but contempt for the woman. His brow furrowed as he looked at her walking away with those eyes so full of questions. Was she for real, he wondered or could she be putting on a good act to cover her crime? She seemed not to know that she had killed someone and he couldn't fathom that anyone could not know. It had been so purposeful as if she wanted to destroy this person under her car. He once again wondered who the victim was and what her relationship was to him.

It took the person from the Department of Criminal Investigation about 90 minutes to arrive. He began to gather evidence as quickly as possible, all business, but it still took another 2 ½ hours before Jacobs and the body were released to go their separate ways, the body to the morgue for an autopsy and he to the hospital.

During that time Debra had been fitted with a collar in case of whiplash, she had been x-rayed and two ribs were found to be broken so she was all taped up and in a hospital gown. "We will keep you here overnight for observation," the doctor told her and he proceeded to assign her a room. When Jacobs arrived, she was dozing in her bed with a constable sitting in a soft chair right beside her.

"Mrs. Wiebe, we need to ask you a few questions," began Detective Sloan, the man who had accompanied Constable Jacobs into the room. "But before we do, we need to read you your rights. Do you understand?"

"Yes, I understand," she said. "Can I call my husband? I left the house in a hurry this morning and we had a big fight."

"Yes you can, as soon as we read you your rights and you have answered a few questions." With that the detective took a card out of his pocket and began to inform Debra that she had the right to an attorney and that she did not have to answer any of the questions posed to her by the officers. "Do you understand these rights as I have read them to you?" asked Sloan.

"Yes but now can I call my husband?"

"Go ahead but then we need to talk," he replied. Debra picked up the phone by her bedside and placed the call.

"Hello, Jerry," she began in a voice that began to show much of the strain she was now under. "Can you come to the hospital? I've been in an accident and they want to keep me overnight for observation."

"Oh my gosh Debra, I knew you shouldn't have driven out of here in the condition you were in." Jerry spoke in a very worried tone of voice. "I'll be right there."

"Now Mrs. Wiebe, exactly what happened?" asked Detective Sloan.

"I'm not sure," she replied. "I left the house this morning very angry but that's all I can remember. Traffic was also very bad this morning with people cutting me off or driving too slow."

"Do you drive fast, Mrs. Wiebe?"

"Not as a rule but as I said I was angry this morning."

"Do you know what happened, any part of it?" he asked again.

"Not really," she stated. "Should I be waiting for a lawyer? Why is that police officer here all the time and why are you asking me all these questions?"

"Mrs. Wiebe, Debra, you killed a man with your car this morning. You rammed him against a brick wall three times and were planning to a fourth time when your car stalled. We have eyewitnesses who say that it appeared to be deliberate on your part. Can you tell us the man's name?"

"I don't understand what you mean by killing someone. I could never kill someone. Did my car go out of control? Did I hit a pedestrian?" Her questions rattled on as if she had just come awake. She felt very confused. What did he mean she had killed someone? She couldn't have. She would have remembered something like that, wouldn't she? What had happened?

Those questions went over and over in her head until she wanted to scream. She was just an ordinary housewife. This kind of thing didn't happen to people like her. Tears started to slide down her cheeks and she rapidly brushed them aside. She hated tears; she always had and besides, crying wouldn't solve anything. She was a survivor. She'd get through this.

"Lord, why are you doing this to me? Hasn't the last four years of testing been enough? I don't want to be a Christian if all it means is more problems." Her thoughts were approaching hysteria as her panic grew and she knew she had to get herself under HER control again. A siren sounded not too far off. "Someone must be sick and on their way to the hospital," she said to no one in particular.

"Did I really kill someone?" she asked again. It just wasn't sinking in. The faces of the police officers in her room were grim. "No I couldn't have!" she answered her own question when no one else seemed to want to. "I want out of here. I want to talk to my husband." She was shouting, clearly becoming more frightened as time went on, and the detective could feel the rumblings of what might be considered compassion for her, for he knew what she was facing over the next few hours or days. He hoped she had a good lawyer.

Screaming, screaming, can't someone shut that woman up? Debra thought. A hand clamped her shoulder tightly and then she realized that she was the one screaming. They tried to calm her but she was so frightened. What was going to happen to her now and where was God when you needed Him? She wanted her husband.

CHAPTER TWO

"You must have really hated this guy. What did he do to you?" The detective was all business, a man in control. However, he could not control the fear that controlled his suspect. The commotion caused by her screaming had brought a nurse into the room to see what had transpired.

"What did you guys do to upset my patient?" she asked. "Leave, or I will call security." With that she ushered the men out of the room.

As they left Detective Sloan added. "I'll leave these questions until a later time when you are feeling better," he said. He and the other police officers left the nurse alone with her patient noticing that she was preparing a hypodermic needle.

Just as she was about to inject her patient, another man walked into the room. "I thought I told you all to leave," she stated emphatically.

"I—I'm her husband," said Jerry. "What are all those police officers doing outside and why are you giving my wife a needle?"

"Your wife has been screaming hysterically, Mr. Wiebe. This will calm her down."

"Honey, I'm here now. Why not try to relax and tell me what happened this morning?"

"All I know is that they tell me I rammed my car into a brick wall killing a man waiting for a bus. I don't remember a thing after I left our street except for lousy drivers. I'm scared Jerry. They think I did this deliberately."

"Now calm down. I think I will get you a lawyer. What do you think?"

"Well…the police officers read me my rights and said I could have one if I wanted before they questioned me. I didn't kill anyone. I couldn't have, could I?"

"Why not let me talk to the detective before I get a lawyer. I'll see what they are talking about." Jerry knew that Debra had been fit to be tied that morning when she had left the house. He also knew that she could have been driving erratically especially considering she had been so very angry that she was almost incoherent. What could have happened between the time she left the house and the time she arrived at the hospital? He had to find out.

When he walked out into the hallway, three pairs of eyes focused on him. He walked up to the first man and asked, "Which one of you is the detective who was just in with my wife?"

"I am Detective Sloan. Who are you?"

"I am Jerry Wiebe, Debra's husband. What happened?"

"That's what we're trying to determine," said Sloan. "But your wife is so out of control that we had to stop all questions. Does she lose it very often?"

"What do you mean lose it? She's just been told that she killed someone. How do you expect her to react?"

"I expect her to answer all our questions as many times as we need to ask them until we determine we understand what happened at that bus stop. Your wife, seen by eyewitnesses, rammed her car deliberately into another man waiting for a bus. It appears that she murdered him in cold blood," said Sloan with a slight rise in blood pressure and tone of voice. "We will leave her alone for now but an officer will remain in the room with her at all times from now on. We will be back in the morning and we will want some answers."

"Well, I intend to get her a lawyer so you will not ask her any questions until that person is here," added Jerry also getting a little angry but feeling more frightened than anything. Could this be true? Jerry returned to sit with Debra for a little while but then he said, "I need to get moving to retain a lawyer before morning. Will you be alright?"

"I feel better than I did a while ago, that's for sure. I'm not sure it's because of the medication or your visit. Jerry, I am so sorry about this morning. Can you ever forgive me?"

"I'll forgive you just like I have all the other times but Debra you have got to get help if we are going to stay together. The kids don't deserve these outbursts especially when they are not the cause of them."

"I know, I know. It's just that I get so mad and then madder still. I'm not sure whether the anger is warranted or not anymore and if it's not, why do I feel it so strongly?"

"We'll deal with this situation first and then the anger management, okay? I'll be back bright and early with a good lawyer. I think you're going to need one."

Debra settled down with her babysitter, the police officer, for the evening after Jerry left but her mind would not let her go to sleep right away. How could all this have happened to her? What had her anger outburst to do with the accident if anything? The questions just piled up in her head until finally, the medication took over and she was able to lapse into a troubled sleep.

The hospital was noisy the next morning with trays clanging and nurses walking or running up and down the halls. The little room where they had placed her was very quiet except for the even breathing of a woman who sat in the chair beside her. "Who are you," she asked.

"I am the police officer who will spend the day with you," the petit blond replied. "Are you hungry enough for breakfast? I am and they promised to bring us both some when you woke up. You didn't sleep too soundly last night so they decided to let you rest as long as you could. Nice of them, huh?"

"Yes, I guess I am a little hungry. Have you seen my husband yet?"

"No, but he called a little while ago to see how you were and to leave you a message that he has secured a good lawyer. He will be here in about a half hour with her."

"Oh my gosh, then I'd better get a move on. Can I get up to comb my hair at least? I also need to use the restroom."

"Sure, as long as you leave the door open a little." Debra winced in pain as she crawled out of bed. While she was feeling somewhat better than she had the night before, her broken ribs were a constant reminder of why she was there. She went into the restroom where she found a comb and a toothbrush with some toothpaste. She had just begun combing her hair when the officer called to her.

"Here is the nurse with your breakfast, Debra. Why not come and eat? You can finish later."

Debra compliantly exited the restroom and moved toward her bed where the nurse had set out a tray with some gray looking cereal in a bowl. Another covered dish contained an egg, a slice of bacon and a slice of toast, not the usual breakfast Debra was accustomed to. But she ate anyway and was soon back repairing the nights tumbled sleep damage to her hair.

When she re-entered her room, she settled down to wait. She waited for her husband and the lawyer he would bring with him. She also waited for this whole nightmare to be over with. The lack of anything to read or look at only lengthened the time she had to think and she didn't want to think about anything right now.

She could still remember the shocked silence that followed her explanation of why she was in the hospital to her husband the night before. They both knew this was the most serious thing they had ever had to face. Her thoughts were in turmoil and one question kept returning to haunt her. What was happening to her?

For some time now, she knew her reactions to certain situations were exaggerated; she overreacted most of the time. But this was different. They claimed she had killed someone deliberately. She didn't know the name of the man she had hit but she was sure she didn't know him personally. The police still hadn't told her who he was. They were assuming she knew.

The door opened abruptly after what seemed like hours but in fact was only a few minutes. Her husband walked rapidly across the room and held his arms out for her to find solace after a long night apart. She had never been so glad to see him in all her life. She snuggled into him for safety and basked in his caring.

Looking over his shoulder was a woman whom Debra assumed was their lawyer. She was reading a file; one that Debra supposed was hers. Her face was grim but she quickly smiled when she noticed that the Wiebe's were looking at her.

"Debra, this is Marcia Dixon. Ms. Dixon, this is my wife, Debra Wiebe." Jerry was relieved he had been able to obtain the services of this high caliber and very capable lawyer. He knew they would have to mortgage the house but his wife was the most important part of his life and he would do anything for her.

"Well, let's see if we can straighten this out, shall we?" The questions began. As Debra told her story, it became evident to Marcia that there were parts missing and she soon became confused as to the sequence of events. The things that the police had in their report did not jive with what Debra was saying so she prodded her about the car ride.

"What were you thinking when you were driving?" she asked.

"I was angry, but determined to get on with my day no matter how tired I was. I hadn't gotten much sleep the night before worrying once again about one of the boys. One was just picked up for DUI so I didn't sleep too soundly." Debra's voice had begun to rise and her lips hardened into a straight line. Telling Marcia was like feeling it all again. This rock in the pit of her stomach was making it's appearance more frequently these days and it was getting harder and harder to regain control over her emotions.

"Tell me, what happened when you hit this man?" Marcia asked.

"I don't know," she replied. "I don't remember much after leaving home other than anger at my family and being frustrated with the traffic. It was like I woke up to find myself in handcuffs. I'm scared, Ms. Dixon. I don't know what's happening to me. Nothing like this has ever happened before. Can you help me?" She was breathing very hard as if she had run some recent race. The feeling, she had, of falling off a high cliff, was evident in the way she clung to the arm of the chair she was sitting in. Her rapid inhaling and exhaling began to indicate her high anxiety level.

"Are you having trouble breathing, Mrs. Wiebe?" Marcia posed the question hoping to allow Debra time to focus on something besides the walls.

"A little, but then I guess you would too, if you woke up one day to find yourself on your way to jail. That is where they will take me, isn't it?" Her gaze traveled over the room and a sense of claustrophobia began to surface. The only furnishings consisted of a small table and two chairs besides the bed she was sitting on. The walls had no pictures on them and there was only one small window. She looked around her and clung to the hand of her husband.

"Of course, you're not going to jail," Jerry jumped in quickly. "Ms Dixon will straighten all this out, won't you?"

"I'm afraid she's right, Jerry. Jail is the next step and she may have to stay there for a while. If I can't convince the judge to drop the charges, and I don't think that's likely with two eye witnesses, then she will have to remain in jail at least until her trial which could take as long as a year to schedule."

"What we have to do now," she continued as she looked at two people who seemed to be back in a state of shock, "is to prepare for the detective's visit this morning. Debra before you answer any question you look at me, I will nod my head to go ahead and answer or shake it in which case you will not answer."

"But Ms. Dixon, aren't you going to be able to get her out on bail at least until the trial?" pleaded Jerry.

"Not on a capital offense and so far, with what the police know, they are considering charging Marcia with first degree murder, definitely a capital offense."

"Boy, I can't believe this," Jerry said as he rubbed his hands through his hair in an attempt to wipe away everything that was happening to them. He considered this situation as happening to them both, not just Debra. That's what marriage was all about, after all.

Marcia continued to prepare and question Debra but Jerry felt the need to escape, to just walk away from the mess they were in for awhile. He decided to offer the three women in the room, which included the silent police officer who had relocated to the hall when Ms. Dixon arrived, some coffee or something and his offer was greedily accepted.

They all wanted a diversion but Marcia wanted her client to be as ready for her next visitors as she could be. She wrote down everything that Debra said to her but Debra's confusion over the events of yesterday morning persisted. Marcia needed to talk to the witnesses first hand and of course, she would have Debra evaluated by a psychiatrist before she could best determine a defense strategy.

Silence followed for a time when Jerry returned with the coffee. It allowed each one to focus on their own thoughts for a while. The Wiebe's were afraid Ms. Dixon was going to suggest that Debra plead guilty and go to jail. Debra figured she would never survive in jail. She needed to have control of her life and in jail, from what she had heard, everyone else was in control of your life. Jerry's thoughts revolved around what he would do if she were incarcerated for any length of time. He would be devastated and he thought about what this would do to the kids, especially the younger two.

A feeling of panic sat just under the surface in Debra's mind, trapping that emotion until it was too great to control. Debra's head ached as these and other thoughts swirled around and around never giving her any peace or answers.

Abruptly, interrupting the silence that surrounded them, the door opened and two burly detectives entered, with a tape recorder under the arm of one of them. They were the same two that had been at the scene of the accident and Detective Sloan said they needed to get her statement.

Marcia placed a reassuring hand on her arm as the detectives set up their equipment. Their first question was to the other occupants in the room. "Who are you and how are you related to the suspect?" Sloan asked, clearly in charge of the interrogation.

Marcia answered first. "I am a lawyer retained by the Wiebes to consult with Mrs. Wiebe during this questioning," she stated.

"I'm her husband," said Jerry.

"You can stay Mr. Wiebe but I want you to remain silent or you will have to leave the room," added the other detective.

"Constable, you can leave for now. Get some coffee or something until we are finished," Sloan referred to the female police officer who shadowed Debra this morning.

"Okay, Mrs. Wiebe, we want you to tell us everything that happened after you left home yesterday morning and please, don't leave out anything," said Detective Sloan who sounded kind in spite of the circumstances. She began slowly and told them about how tired she was and her delivery of perfume products. She talked about the crazy drivers and her anger but then she stopped.

"What can you tell us about the man you hit. Where had you met him before?" Detective Jones was not as chivalrous and his voice had a cruel note to it. He stared at her as she hesitated.

"I don't know him at all. In fact, I don't know what his name is or what he looks like." She began to tremble then, and she suddenly felt so cold.

"Come on, Mrs. Wiebe. Are you trying to tell us that you deliberately hit a stranger for no reason whatsoever?" Jones sneered, clearly not believing Debra's insistence that she was not aware of who this man could be. "Why were you so angry with him that you raced your car up on the sidewalk and then twice rammed him against a brick wall? Come on, Mrs. Wiebe. Was he your lover? Did he cheat on you? What was your relationship with him?" Jones fairly shouted the last question making Debra teary eyed and fearful. Sloan cautioned him to take it easy and Marcia added that she would instruct her client to not answer any more questions if his attitude persisted.

They allowed Jerry to put his arms around her to comfort her but it didn't seem to help. She was thankful they had allowed him to be there with her. He was her best friend. In fact since her girlfriend had moved to the coast, he was her only friend. The trembling lessened so she continued. "It was an accident that I killed him. My car must have gone out of control or something. I could never kill anyone." She wanted to cry but that lump was back and she had a hard time swallowing.

"The man's name is Derrick Johnson. He's a student at the college and was on his way to school. Are you sure you didn't know him from some bar or through your children? Maybe he was a friend of theirs and since you were so angry with them, you took it out on Derrick. Come on Mrs. Wiebe, why did you kill him?" Detective Jones was beginning to scare her even more. They really thought she could deliberately kill someone. This had to be some kind of a nightmare.

"I didn't know him and I didn't do this on purpose. My car went out of control," she shouted at them, this time loosing her temper. Who did they think she was anyway, some lower class person? She was a Christian after all and abided by the Ten Commandments. She didn't even swear or drink or smoke. Her life was not so nice these days but she still wasn't a murderer. She had to get them to see that.

"Mr. Johnson had been standing by that bus stop, minding his own business, then. Is that correct, Debra?" asked detective Sloan. "If that is so, then you, willfully and with intent, rammed him with your car, 3 or 4 times. You were witnessed in the act by," he took out his notebook, "a Mister Franco and a Miss Delbridge who were waiting for the same bus as Mr. Johnson. They saw you hit the man the first time, back up a second time and then try a third time to hit Johnson and then the wall. From Mr. Franco's viewpoint, it was deliberate and Miss Delbridge corroborates his story exactly. Can you explain that, Debra?" He was watching her face as he detailed what she had done but only her blank look stared back at him.

"I don't know anything about that man or hitting him, if that is what I did." Tears started to flow as the full import of his words sank in for the first time. She had actually killed someone. Never before had she felt this kind of fear.

Marcia asked the detectives what the charge would be and they said that they were charging her with 'First Degree Premeditated Murder' and they planned to transport her to the police station right away, as soon as she was dressed.

"You'll be finger printed, photographed, and placed in a cell until your hearing later in the day." Marcia explained after the detectives left the room. Debra was sobbing in Jerry's arms but she continued.

"I'll look into the bail arrangement but as I told you earlier, there probably won't be any bail allowed. I will also waive a speedy trial since I want to have you examined by a psychiatrist. Don't worry, Debra, we'll get this all sorted out." Marcia hated to leave her there but there was no other choice. Until they discovered the truth, she would have to stand against these charges.

"Do you think I did it deliberately, Ms. Dixon? I couldn't have. I'm not like that," she pleaded with her counsel to help her and to believe in her.

"My job is not to pass judgment but to give you the best defense I can. However, for some odd reason, I do believe you. I just have to find a way to prove that you were unaware of your actions at the time of the incident. Now, you get dressed. I'll leave you and Jerry here for a time to say good-bye and then I'll come with you to the police station, okay."

Debra looked at her husband. He had been silent throughout this whole ordeal except to fold her in his arms when she needed him but now she needed him to say something. Jerry was a good husband and they had a good marriage in spite of all the arguments lately. Most of those had been because of the kids and his trusting attitude. Now she hoped his trusting attitude was on her side.

"If ever there was a time to ask for the Lord's help, it's now," he said. "I know you couldn't kill anyone but until they discover the truth, that's what they believe. Come here, honey." He held out his arms for her and she went to her safe place. His arms had always made her feel safe as no one else or no other place ever had in her lifetime. Her tears were mixed with his as they separately and yet together contemplated their dilemma.

"Lord," he prayed, "You promised you would not give us more than we can handle. We are grabbing unto that promise right now. Please help us to know what really happened and help Marcia as she prepares to defend Debra.

Please help the judge to grant bail so we can get Debra out of jail quickly and, Father, please give us the strength to go through this trial. Amen."

Their beliefs were strong or so they thought. They couldn't imagine someone going through this without God. Debra wasn't too sure anymore if God was really on their side but she knew there was a God and even if she was angry with Him, Jerry wasn't. Trusting in God completely meant very little to her, as she really didn't understand what that kind of trust meant.

Their five minutes were up and the detectives refused to let Jerry go with her to booking. She felt like a child being separated from a parent. She was so frightened. As they led her away, Jerry smiled at her and told her to be brave.

"I'll be down to the police station to see you as soon as they will let me, honey, and Marcia will work at getting you out of there. See you later," he shouted down the hallway, as Debra was escorted in hand cuffs again toward the elevator and past hundreds of staring eyes. He hoped this terrible situation wouldn't last too long since Debra's moods were not too predictable anymore. "She must get some quality sleep soon," he thought," or she's going to have a nervous breakdown".

CHAPTER THREE

Recognizing her as a first time offender, the policemen tried to be as kind as they could during the process of booking their suspect, but the whole ordeal was still very traumatic to Debra. Nothing they could say or do could take away her pain and sense of shock over what had occurred. She had killed someone. To her, what she was undergoing was secondary to the trauma she had caused the family of that boy.

She was frightened, but they had lost a son and a brother. Not only had she killed him but she had been so brutal about it. Her senses were overwhelming and in such a turmoil. Part of her wanted to run and hide where she would not have to deal with all this and the other part felt the electric chair would be too good for her.

Feelings of guilt she was used to, as most of her life she had felt guilty over something or other. While she had never been a child who caused trouble, her memories of childhood were of her father looking down his nose at her with judgment in his eyes, as if she were the biggest mistake of his life. She couldn't remember ever feeling as if he loved her-just that he was unhappy with her.

Many times, she received punishment due her brother or sister because her father or mother assumed she was the culprit whether in a fight of when one of her siblings broke something or lost something. It somehow always ended up being her fault.

No matter how hard she tried to please her dad, she always felt that she had done something wrong. It had taken her many years to overcome the notion that if her own father couldn't love her, it must be because she didn't deserve to be loved. Her husband's patient love for her had helped with her healing process, but at times of insecurity, such as today, those old feelings of being guilty and unlovable rushed back with a vengeance. Certainly she felt she must deserve the treatment she was now receiving.

After the booking procedure was completed, Debra was ushered into a small room where she was told to undress. A large matronly female guard came in and proceeded to search every body cavity she had. Debra was never so humiliated in her life. Her only experiences of nudity with someone other than her husband were with her gynecologist and during childbirth. After ensuring there was nothing hidden on or within her body, she was led into another room where a shower stall permitted a very cold shower. Once she had shivered under the tap for a few minutes, she dried herself with a scratchy towel and then she was sprinkled with some white powder.

"What's that for?" she sputtered.

"Lice," the matron said, smirking as she noticed the look of revulsion on Debra's face. She was then given a bright orange jumpsuit to wear over some generic cotton underwear that scratched her skin as soon a she put them on. The matron was not as solicitous as the male police officers had been. She treated Debra as if she was already guilty.

When they walked down a flight of stairs to the cellblock, Debra could feel her panic returning once again. Why was this happening to her? She was basically a good person. Metal bars, metal locks, and metal keys all clanged together to make a deafening sound as her cell door was slammed shut, leaving her alone for the first time all day. Those bars held her in place. She could no longer come and go as she pleased. Before long claustrophobia began to set in and the scream she had held in place all day erupted in full force.

"Calm down in there," said the jailor, a man who sat at the end of the row of cells. "Or I'll come over there and beat it out of you."

"Hon," a voice came from the cell beside Debra's. "Trust me-you don't want to cause any trouble with these guys. Their idea of discipline ain't pretty. Try to think about something, anything other than those bars. It'll help some. Here's a good book to read if you want," she added as she slid a book through the bars of her cell and over to the bars blocking Debra's passage to freedom.

Debra, suddenly frightened as she imagined the possibilities of what an angry jailor could do, settled down on her bunk with the Bible but not opening it yet, knowing she could never concentrate long enough to get anything out of it. Sitting in this cell, with no way out, but no privacy either, reminded her of what it had been like the time she baby-sat for that couple when she was fifteen.

It had been dark outside and the only curtains on the multitude of windows were sheer. She felt as if the entire world could see her but she couldn't see them; like being naked and exposed to watching evil eyes. She had tried different things to trick her mind into not being afraid, but it seemed that the more she tried not to think about it, the more she became aware of how vulnerable she was to those eyes. In the end, all she could do was hope they would be home soon.

That same sense of fear was present now and it was thick and touchable. She knew these days that Satan was the author of fear and he always knew when to exercise his options. Somehow, though, that knowledge did not comfort her here. God seemed so far away and yet the Bible said he cared for all his creatures, even the little sparrow.

"Get thee behind me Satan and I command you with the blood of Jesus to go from here," she repeated several times. She knew Satan's choices over her were limited when she commanded him this way and it always helped to reassure her of who really was in control of her life and the world. Somehow God would see her through this. As she prayed, she felt herself begin to unwind, and felt her breathing become steadier again. Then she started to pray for the boy's family.

She remained quiet, in prayer, for some time, praying for his soul and the family. She prayed that he was a believer for then he would be in a better place. She worshipped God as best she could although it was hard to keep her tension about that place from intruding into her thoughts. The time passed so slowly and it seemed hours since she had been brought here.

"Mrs. Wiebe, your lawyer's here to brief you on your hearing so please step back while I open the door." She jumped when the voice suddenly intruded into her quietness. The guards were very impersonal souls but then she supposed that they had a lot of people go through these cells.

They escorted Debra to another small room with a table in the center and two chairs. Marcia was waiting for her and she smiled as she saw her. Debra's heart quickened. Here was someone familiar, someone who cared whether she was here or not and someone who would get her out of this.

"When can I go home?" she asked Marcia. Debra clutched at her jacket sleeve with that look of pleading in her eyes and Marcia felt so sorry for her. This was not going to be easy.

"The charge against you is very serious," Marcia began. "I would like you to agree to an evaluation by a psychiatrist to see if we can consider a plea of not guilty by reason of insanity. There are so many unanswered questions about your memory blackout and what happened between the time you left home and the time the accident occurred. Being angry just simply isn't a good enough reason to do what you did, and I feel we need some help to establish more facts."

Marcia continued. "For this type of crime, if you are found guilty at trial, you could be looking at life in a maximum security prison with no time off for good behavior. The police will do everything they can to tie you to the victim and if they succeed, they will win their case of premeditation. That is, of course, the worst case scenario."

"I believe you when you say you knew nothing of this man so that makes you temporarily insane at the time of the accident by the definition of the law. A conversation with someone in the psychiatric community about your loss of memory can only help us. I know it's not uncommon for a person to be so traumatized that they suffer a memory loss," she added, "but I still don't understand why it happened at all. They'll be calling us soon. Once we enter your not guilty plea, the judge will send you for evaluation at the psychiatric facility in Clarkville for a minimum of thirty days. That will determine if you are sane or not and competent to stand trial. They will find you sane, of course. I know a doctor there, or at least he was still there the last time I talked with him. A few sessions with him may shed some light on this whole mess. In the meantime, here are some magazines and I'll be back just before you're called into court tomorrow."

Debra just stared in shock. As many times as she heard the seriousness of her situation she could not get over the fact that Marcia was saying she could go to prison but now to a psychiatric hospital as well. She felt like she had left her body and was standing in the room listening for someone else. She wanted to pull into herself as far as she could go and never leave. Without a word, she sat down and just stared at the floor.

Another scream started low, deep in her soul, where she usually tried to keep her emotions. She screamed and screamed until the guards finally came. They quickly assessed her hysteria and shook her hard to calm her. Debra didn't think she would ever feel calm and peace again.

"Debra!" Marcia shouted at her. "You've got to calm down. We need you to stay in control so you can tell us anything that comes to your mind about the accident. Please, Debra, listen to me!" she pleaded. "You've still got a husband who loves you very much and although, he too, doesn't understand what's happened, he knows you could never deliberately kill someone."

"Your children still need you to be calm so you can help them through this. Snap out of it, Debra and get strong!" Marcia commanded. "Get angry if you have to, but don't fall apart on me. I need you to help me defend you." Marcia watched as Debra's panic subsided. She took a deep breath and so did her client. This woman was strong and she was a survivor. Marcia had never hoped for anything more than that right now. She also hoped the doctor at the psychiatric hospital would prescribe some tranquilizers as soon as Debra arrived.

"Are you going to be okay, for now?" she asked. "I need to make some phone calls. You're allowed a visitor. Would you like Jerry to come in for a while? He can only stay for half an hour but it'll give you a reason to be strong. If you fall apart so will he. Are you okay?" She looked at Debra with caring written all over her and Debra slowly nodded her head. "I'll be back as soon as I can. See you soon." She was gone.

Debra took slow deep breaths and waited for her best friend. She hated for Jerry to see her here but she needed him so much. Footsteps fast approaching made her turn towards the door of this small room with these visible, invisible walls. There were a few other prisoners somewhere close to her for she could hear other doors opening and other angry words but she was immersed in her own world of pain.

When Jerry entered the room, she ran toward him but the guard who let him in cautioned them to remain separated. Neither said a word for a few minutes. Jerry smiled trying to remain strong for her and he could tell she was making an effort for him too. When Marcia had passed him in the hall, she had explained how Debra had fallen apart once again. She also suggested that Jerry find her some tranquilizers, that the prison would allow her to have one or two a day. They would bring them to her of course. Marcia said the pills needed to be strong but not so much as to diminish Debra's thought processes any further.

The Wiebe's knew their family would survive. They were committed to their marriage and to each other. Divorce was not a part of their vocabulary. With God's help, they would survive this test just as they had others in the past.

The half hour was over before either realized it. They had spent time in prayer and in reminiscing about the good parts of their family. Debra spoke of the birth of each of their children and the love that flowed from her heart as each had been added to their family. She knew that hate was not the word she would describe her relationship to any of them but when she was really angry as she had been that morning, she felt hate almost like a tangible thing.

Her children had taught her so much over the years. Each had a strength that made the family stronger but they also had weaknesses that caused them to rely on one another. When the two older ones began to rebel, it took Jerry and Debra by surprise because they thought they had a good relationship with their kids. They thought that they communicated as a family really well and that rebellious teenagers were not part of their future. How wrong they had been.

But nevertheless, Debra and Jerry still loved all four. They knew that, once again with God's help, the family would be whole...some day. Debra had scrap booked many great memories of the children's growing up years, which also reflected their growth as parents. Although they were not perfect, they had improved over the years.

Each time a test came their way, they knew they had two choices, try to do things entirely on their own or seek God's help. They had also discovered over the years that when looking at a problem or situation with God's perspective, that situation or problem became much smaller and more manageable.

Debra and Jerry also had time to reflect on the fun times, and there were many over the years, when they had vacationed with the family or just by themselves or when they had spent some time after marriage dating, visiting with friends, or just having a cozy night at home. All these memories helped to strengthen them now and Debra resolved to continue her reflections when she returned to her cell.

When her guard came to take her back to her cell and after she said good-bye to Jerry, he escorted her past the cell of the woman who had passed her the book, a book she had not even looked at yet. She thanked her in passing but the woman did not acknowledge her presence. The guard poked her with his stick. "No talking to the other prisoners while you are moving down this corridor, lady," he barked.

Debra just hung her head. There were so many rules. How was she ever going to know them all? Maybe after the guard left, she could see if the woman next door would visit for a while.

Clang, clang, clang. Metal on metal and then the emptiness of confinement. Would she ever get used to this? The guard walked back to his station and once he was out of earshot, Debra whispered, "Hi there, remember me?"

"Sure. What do you want?"

"Are we allowed to talk now? There are so many rules I don't know," Debra explained.

"Sure. Whata ya wanna know?"

"What's your name? My name is Debra."

"I'm Suzette. And yes it's okay to talk now just not when they are transporting us from one area of the prison to another. What're ya in for?"

"Hi Suzette," answered Debra. "It's good to have someone to talk to. I am charged with first degree murder but I'm not guilty," she added.

"Ya sure. That's what they all say. Who'd ya kill anyway?"

"My car must have gone out of control, and it hit a young man at a bus stop."

"Well isn't that just a traffic accident?"

"Apparently not since I am supposed to have deliberately ran up on the sidewalk to kill him," Debra explained, "but I don't remember doing it."

"Oh-h-h-h...Let's change the subject. Do ya have family?" And with that question a long conversation began. Suzette also had four kids, younger than Debra's but she was raising them with a father who spent most of his time elsewhere getting drunk. "Now that I'm in jail, they are being looked after by some people from my church."

"Oh...Are you a Christian?"

"Didn't you see the book I gave you? It's a Bible. That book has helped me through many a dreary night in here and has also comforted me when I worry about my kids. You need to read it and you will be able to handle anything they throw at you, even a life sentence, if it comes to that."

"I don't even want to think about that. I'm going to read this tonight. Thanks for the help. By the way, what are they holding you for if that's not too personal?"

"I hit my old man over the head with a 2 x 4 the last time he tried to beat on me. He ended up in the hospital and they charged me with spousal abuse. Can ya believe it?"

"Have you had a trial yet?"

"Heck no! I'll be here for six months or more before they get around to deciding my fate. I'm gonna lay down for a short snooze," added Suzette. "Talk to ya later."

And with that Debra lay down on her bunk, turned on her little light, and began to read the Bible Suzette had given her. She decided to begin where all new believers usually begin who want to know more about the Lord…in the book of John. Although she had been a Christian for a long time, she felt that she had the time to start from the beginning again. She read until she was able to fall asleep and in her dreams God was her protector and comforter once more.

CHAPTER FOUR

The arraignment hearing began later the next day but sooner than they had planned. However, Marcia was ready. The judge was all business and his brusque manner intimidated Debra. She took a few more deep breaths. Jerry was sitting just behind them and when the Judge asked the involved councils to speak, it sounded just like all the TV programs she had ever watched. First the prosecuting attorney spoke and then Marcia. The prosecuting attorney indicated that they felt they had sufficient evidence to win their case and that she was definitely a flight risk since her behavior was already considered erratic and peculiar.

Marcia spoke strongly of Debra's family; the reason she was not a flight risk. She also reminded the judge that her client had not ever committed a crime of any kind before. The judge then asked Debra what plea she was going to enter and Marcia replied that her client would plead not guilty by reason of temporary insanity. The judge then ordered Debra to be placed in Clarkville Psychiatric Hospital until such time as it could be determined if she was sane and competent to stand trial. This was really not a surprise to anyone, however.

The judge complied with Marcia's petition to waive a speedy trial. As Jerry watched, he noticed that Debra had a haunted look throughout the hearing. When she looked towards the parents of the boy she had killed, he watched as she crumbled even further into her seat. How will she...we ever live through this, he asked himself. But he knew in his heart that they could and they would.

The children's faces were the hardest to see in this courtroom. Debra felt she had disappointed them and let them down. Both had tears in their eyes when she reached toward them for a hug after the proceedings were over. Jerry smiled though and reassured them all that they would get through this. He told Debra that he would visit as often as he could and that together they would fight the charges brought against her.

The bailiff took her by the arm and led her back to her cell in the lower level of the courthouse building, which also housed the police station. The metal grinding metal of the doors opening and closing were beginning to sound familiar if not comforting. Once she was back in her cell, her neighbor asked, "How did it go?"

"They're sending me to a place called Clarkville for evaluation," she answered. "Those prosecuting attorneys sounded so angry and so sure I am a devil in disguise that I am really scared they will win their case even though I know that I could never have deliberately done something like this."

"That's the way they all sound when they think they're right," replied Suzette. "You just keep thinking about any piece of information you can give your attorney to help her fight for you and keep on reading that Bible I gave you."

"I asked Jerry, my husband, to bring mine from home so I can give you this one back," stated Debra.

"Oh, that's okay. Take as long as you need. I have a lot of verses memorized so I just keep saying them over and over to myself. They are almost the same as reading the book for myself."

"Jerry promised to visit later today and he will bring it then."

"Well great then. You have something to look forward to. My old man never comes and he never brings me the kids for a visit. It gets lonely sometimes."

Debra couldn't wait to see her kids and Jerry, of course. But she hadn't spent anytime with her two youngest since leaving home two days ago. She settled down on her bunk to wait until visiting hours at four o'clock that afternoon. It felt like she had been away from home for a lot longer than two days.

Debra had given birth to her youngest son and daughter a few years after her first two sons were born. Although they were still quite young, they were old enough to understand how their older brothers rebellion had affected the family and were cautious about being "good". They tried really hard to do what was expected of them and for the most part they succeeded but Debra knew that her older children had also behaved pretty well at that age as well.

When the other two left, tension in the house had lessened to some extent but the parent's constant worry over their older boys left the younger siblings in need of some attention themselves. Debra loved the time they spent together going to school each morning since this allowed her some quality time with them. She missed that time over the last two days.

During her visit to the courtroom, the authorities had provided her with lunch since she had had to wait so long for her turn before the judge. Now, however, she felt the need for something to snack on and she was dying for a hot cup of coffee. Being in this place, however, took away her freedom to just get up and get whatever she wanted when she wanted it.

Debra felt tears puddle and then drip from her lower eyelids. It was very easy to feel sorry for oneself in this place she was discovering. Forced to remain in her cell behind locked doors made her feel as if she no longer had any control over her life. Other people told her when she could go to the restroom, when she could eat, and when she could sleep. They controlled when she had visitors and how long they could stay. They even controlled how often she changed her underwear or showered.

The tears were building to the point where Debra was literally sobbing into her pillow, a thing she had not ever done unless her anger made her so mad she had no other outlet. Tears had always been a sign of weakness to Debra but now…

"Wiebe, you have a visitor." A guard spoke right outside her cell. "Pull yourself together and come with me."

"I-I d-d-don't even h-h-have a Kleenex in h-h-here," she sobbed.

"Make a list and give it to your husband. He can bring you most anything as long as the guards at the entrance permit him to. They have to search him each time he comes anyway."

"Oh-h-n-n-no, why do they have to s-s-search my h-h-husband? He's done n-n-nothing wrong."

"It's just routine, Wiebe. Now quit your blubbering and wipe those tears on a sleeve or something. Let's get moving. I haven't got all day." Debra almost thought that maybe his harsh attitude was all a charade but she was afraid to ask in case it wasn't. She sniffed and wiped her nose and her eyes on the sleeve of her jumpsuit. The material scratched but was just what she needed to get herself under control.

The guard opened the door to her cell and they began the short walk to the visitor's room, where she had seen Jerry earlier. Everything in this place could use some brightening up, she thought as they walked. They must have had a sale on gray paint. Boy, was that humor returning?

When Jerry saw her tear streaked face, his smile disappeared. "Ah-h-h, honey? It'll be okay?" he said in as soothing a voice as he could. Debra moved swiftly into his arms without thinking.

"Keep your distance, you two," yelled the guard who would monitor their visit.

"Oh right, no touching," Jerry complied.

"I feel so alone in here," said Debra after they were seated across from each other at the table in the center of the room. "I put myself here and I deserve everything that happens."

"Sh-h-h...don't talk like that Debra. The guard might overhear and take that as an admission of guilt."

"Well they have people who saw what I did so I must have done it. I am having a really hard time here, trying to fathom that I actually killed someone and the way I did it. Oh, Jerry could I be that rotten inside?"

"Honey, not one of us knows how we will react in any given situation. Look at all the road rage they talk about now. Something happened to you and we're going to get to the bottom of this. You can do this, Debra. You're a strong woman."

"I wanted a cup of coffee and I realized that I couldn't just get up and get one. Someone else controls every facet of my life in here and I have no say over it. You know how I like to be in control."

"God is in control and you need to rely on Him to get you through all this. Maybe this will be an opportunity for you to learn to lean on Him more fully instead of your own abilities as you have in the past," added Jerry.

"Harrumph! I suppose so. Where are the kids? I thought you were going to bring them with you this time."

"They wouldn't let the kids inside. They have to be over eighteen to visit." As Jerry saw tears once more in his wife's eyes he quickly added, "They can write though and they can also send you little gifts. What are some of the things you need in here?"

Debra quickly swiped at her eyes with her sleeve and sniffed her nose. "The guard said you could bring just about anything here but they will search everything. They don't make you undress to search you, do they?"

"No, they just pat me up and down. It's not so bad. Now what do you need?"

CHAPTER FIVE

Shortly after Jerry left for home to gather the list of supplies Debra needed and with a promise to return bright and early the next morning, Marcia Dixon drove into the parking lot at the courthouse. She walked through the front door, down the hallway and took the nearest elevator to the jail adjacent to the police station.

"I need to see my client, Debra Wiebe," she said to the first person she encountered at the jail.

"Certainly Ms. Dixon. Come this way." And with that Marcia was taken to a small room, much smaller than the visitor room where her purse and briefcase were searched before she was left alone to wait for Debra.

A few minutes later a door opened on the opposite side of the room and in walked her client with her guard almost physically attached. "Can you leave us alone, please?" Marcia asked. "I am her lawyer."

"Right, but don't take too long or she won't get any supper. It's served in 30 minutes," he groused.

Marcia and Debra hugged for the first time. Debra was so happy to see someone so soon after Jerry left. Anything to keep her out of that cell, she thought.

"How's it going?" Marcia began.

"Not so bad now," said Debra. "Jerry just left and he promised he'd be here early with some things I need."

"That's good because they will probably transport you around noon."

"That soon. Will Jerry be able to visit me there and what about the kids? They won't let them come in here."

"The atmosphere at the hospital is a little more relaxed so I think that visitors of all ages are allowed and you won't be locked in a cell either," explained Marcia.

"The sooner we can get started on finding out why the events of the other day happened, the better. I plan to talk to someone I know, a counselor, who might be willing to see you for some extended therapy after the doctors at the hospital have determined your mental state."

"Can you find me a Christian counselor?" asked Debra.

"Why Christian?" asked Marcia

"I am a Christian and I would feel better if the person I am talking to understood where I was coming from," her client replied.

"I'll see what I can do. In the meantime, sit tight. I'll come back as soon as I have more information. The police will be doing whatever they can to tie you to this man. Without that they don't have a capital case."

"Well, I don't know him, never knew him and only wish I had never…k-k-k-illed him either," Debra stammered emphatically.

"I know," Marcia added, "and I'm going to prove that you did not know what you were doing when it happened either. Take it easy. I'll see you soon." Marcia left the same way she had come and got into her car. As she pulled away from the parking lot she thought to herself, "Now my work will begin in earnest."

There had to be some way to keep this woman from spending time in a facility meant for criminals, for no matter what Debra had or had not done, Marcia would never believe she was a murderer. There had to be a reason why all this happened and she was going to find it. Once the confusion over what really went through Debra's mind that morning was settled, she would be able to assemble the defense witnesses needed to bring the jury to the same conclusions she had reached. She would begin by talking to all of the close acquaintances of the Wiebe's, and the people who attended church with them. "Right now though," she decided, "I want to talk to the two remaining children in the Wiebe household."

With that, she headed toward the end of town where the Wiebe home was located. On the way, her mind returned to the woman whose case she had agreed to defend. What kind of person would run over someone whom she had never met before? Debra seemed to be not only stable but also an average homemaker. She appeared to have some emotional problems but in no way could that explain what had happened, could it?

The traffic, light for that time of day, thinned even more the closer Marcia came to Westview. The suburb consisted of moderately priced homes, a school for elementary aged children, and a couple of those man-made lakes every new developer built to satisfy the government's needs for green space. The neighborhood, quiet by any city's standards, seemed a great place to raise a family to Marcia's inexperienced eye about such matters.

When she pulled into the driveway, the Wiebe's little Shih-Tzu began to bark through the big picture window at the front of the house heralding her arrival to everyone inside. Josie, a six year old in pigtails and her older brother Tom answered the ring of their doorbell a minute or two later. When Marcia explained who she was, they invited her in and asked if they could take her coat.

Polite, she noticed. "Can we sit down to talk for a minute?" she asked.

"What about?" they both answered her question with one of their own.

"Your mom."

"W-e-l-l-l, I don't know if we should talk to you when our Dad isn't home. Especially about mom," replied thirteen-year-old Tom, a little wiser than he should have to be for his age. "Oh-h I think I hear his car now."

Both children got up quietly and moved toward the front door, which opened just as they got there. "Dad, Ms. Dixon wants us to talk to her about Mom. Is that okay?" Tom jumped on his father as soon as he had gotten all the way through the door.

"O-h-h, hi Marcia. I thought I recognized your car. What can we do to help?" Jerry greeted his wife's attorney.

"Well I thought I would have a little more information to give a counselor if I talk to the kids first. I plan to talk to one as soon as I can get an appointment."

"If it will help their mother, go right ahead. Want some coffee? Jerry asked. "I was going to make a cup for myself anyway."

"Sure, Jerry that would be great. Now kids, lets begin." And the conversation over the next half hour expanded Marcia's picture of her client to a very great extent. The kids were honest and their evaluation of their mother held concern and love all in the same breathe.

"Will you be able to free our mom," asked Josie. Tears came quickly to the surface when she contemplated the thought of her mother behind bars. Having only seen quick glimpses of prison on TV, Josie knew it was not a great place for their mother to be.

"We'll do the best we can," Marcia assured the little girl.

"Quit being such a cry baby," rebuked her brother. "Mom and Dad will look after everything. They always do. Isn't that right Ms. Dixon?" asked Tom with a plea for reassurance in his too old voice.

"We'll all do the best we can," repeated Marcia once again. "But for now, you need to ask God to take care of your mother. Right Jerry?"

"That's right kids. Now let's let Ms. Dixon get on her way so she can get some rest for a big day tomorrow."

Marcia said a quick good-bye to this family whose life had changed so drastically in so short a time. She got into her car and then sat for a moment wondering how they would all handle it if their mother had to be imprisoned for a long period of time. She resolved to do the best she could not to let that happen. She put the car in gear and backed down the driveway.

For some reason, this case was becoming more important than it probably should be. She pointed her car homeward and then let the case take over again. She really wanted to see Debra reunited with her family. The woman was so lucky but she didn't seem to know that. She was so strung out over her rebellious teens that she hardly noticed these younger two who themselves noticed her lack of attention. Marcia hoped that would change. If only…

Marcia was a slim woman in her early thirties. She had never married since her career had always taken precedence in her life but her career was stable now and sometimes she wished she had someone at home to talk over her cases with. Forget the cases, she just wanted someone to talk to at the end of the day. She longed for the relationship that Debra was jeopardizing by her angry outbursts.

Marcia's dark good looks caused many to turn in her direction whenever she was out and about but she was oblivious to it all, her mind always occupied with the case at hand.

"I wonder if Samantha would be a good person to think out loud with," she wondered. "I think I'll give her a call and we can have dinner together." Samantha was a close friend and in this case a much needed voice to help her understand the faith aspect of her client.

The call was made from the cellular phone in her automobile and the two friends agreed to meet at their favorite dining spot over by the man-made lake in the suburb where they both lived. The scenery from the window of the restaurant would offer a relaxing diversion from their day.

"Okay, out with it," began Samantha as soon as they were seated. Samantha was a forty five year old woman who was a little more religious than Marcia liked but was someone she knew she could count on. "I know this is not just a social call."

"I'm sorry. I guess I haven't been exactly sociable lately. You're right, I do have a client I need to understand better and I think you can help," Marcia began. "She claims to be Christian. She sounds the same as you when it comes to her beliefs."

"Being a Christian is not the same as being religious, you know," replied Samantha as soon as the waiter left with their order. "Being a Christian is a way of life. It reflects in our daily life just as the difference between being educated or not. Let me explain," she added when she saw the puzzled look on her friend's face. "A person who has a university degree behaves and reacts to life differently than someone who has only a 6th grade education, wouldn't you agree? Well it's the same with a person who is a true Christian compared to one who is religious. A true believer, a Christian, walks through life with Christ in mind, following His example while a religious person walks through life trying on his own to live a good life because she believes that is what is expected of her. A true Christian while she may make mistakes, also knows that there is nothing she can do to be good enough for God by herself so has committed her life to living with Christ as part of her person, allowing the Holy Spirit to dictate her path through life. Does that make sense to you?"

"I guess that would explain why my client would want a counselor who is also Christian," said Marcia. "Only another Christian could understand what you just said."

The two friends were soon immersed in the details of Marcia's latest case. Marcia had always been able to discuss her cases with this friend without fearing that Samantha would ask her questions she could not answer because of client confidentiality.

"Why not try asking the people at Christian Counseling Center for some answers. They deal mostly with people from Christian homes and they may know more about the psyche of someone such as you describe," offered Samantha.

"I didn't even know that a Christian counseling center existed. Do you know anyone who works there?" Samantha shook her head and Marcia once again thought it was strange that people from a church background felt the need for a specialized counselor.

But she was willing to give anything a try in order to help her client and of course win her case. "Wait here while I make an appointment and then we can talk of something more pleasant for the rest of our dinner."

As she sauntered to the pay phone in the lobby of the restaurant, she chuckled, thinking of the many times she and Samantha had tried to relax. With the two of them having such high-pressure jobs, those times were few and far between. Samantha was an ad executive for the Walker Agency, one of the most prestigious advertising agencies in the city, in fact in their whole state. She worked long hours with deadlines to reach all the time.

Although, older than Marcia, the two had become acquainted about ten years before when Marcia, as part of her internship for law school, had sat in on the discussion with Samantha's lawyer about her divorce case. Samantha's divorce was finalized about a year later and by then, the two had become fast friends. Marcia either called her or Samantha took the initiative for a get-together at least once a month since then. Sometimes last minute cancellations were necessary but the friendship still flourished.

The appointment at the Christian counseling center was quickly made with a woman by the name of Mary. Marcia made a quick detour to the restroom before returning to their table. "Did you get an appointment at the center?" asked Samantha.

"Yes I did and they could see me right away tomorrow morning. They must not have very many clients," added Marcia. "I hope they are good. My client is going to need to talk to someone who is very professional and can help clear up all the confusion about her blackout yesterday. Let's forget about this case, though, for the rest of the evening. I want to hear how you've been and what you've been up to."

Samantha and Marcia spent the rest of the evening enjoying pleasant conversation over a tasty meal with no interruptions, a luxury neither of them often had, to be sure. When Marcia left the restaurant, she headed straight home, with a plan to get to bed as soon as she could so her mind would be well rested for the next day. Meeting with a

Christian counselor would be a first for her and she wanted to make sure that she evaluated the person's ability in light of her client's needs correctly.

CHAPTER SIX

The office of the Christian Counseling Center was located in the opposite end of the city from Marcia's office but was easy to find and the parking was plentiful. She walked into a cool, restful atmosphere decorated in calming shades of grays and pinks.

As Victoria, the receptionist, ushered her into the counselor's office, Marcia shook hands with a woman of indeterminate age who appeared to be, at first glance, a very caring person. She had the warmest smile Marcia had seen in a long while with the ability to put one at ease immediately. Mary indicated a seat for Marcia and then proceeded to ask how she could help her.

"I have a client, a Christian woman, who ran over a pedestrian a couple of days ago in a seemingly deliberate manner. According to the police report and the eyewitness account, she backed her car up again and again to run over this person, a man whom she claims never to have seen before. Can you give me some insight into what would make a person, someone who has never had any involvement with the police except for a parking ticket or

76

speeding ticket, do such a thing?" Marcia hoped she was not telling this woman too much but she wanted her to be clear about her client. "Oh, and I almost forgot. She talks about an overwhelming anger just before the incident and she really can't remember what she did."

"Does this woman have a history of abuse either now or in childhood? What kind of husband does she have and do you know if she was ever raped?" Mary was a trained therapist and her questions were probing. "I would need to know a lot more about her before I could make an accurate assessment."

"I don't know a lot about her life but I do know that their teens have been giving them a hard time. They've been doing some pretty unusual things considering the kind of life they've led." Marcia was quick to explain that she thought that her clients had been good parents, at least according to her conversation earlier with their youngest children. Yet their older children seemed to be rebelling to such a degree that the whole family had been in turmoil for a couple of years now.

"I'm not sure that explains your clients bizarre behavior," Mary stated. "A lot of kids act out and their

Moms don't go out and run someone over. I would need to know even more before I could judge the character of this individual. Could you tell me about her temper? Does she have one and how does it manifest itself? Has she ever hit the kids in anger or lost it when she's disciplining any one of them? Does she drink or do drugs? These are all things I need to know".

"As I told you she's a Christian, the born again kind. You know...really straight. I think, Jerry told me, she smoked a long time ago but as for drinking, she only has one once in a blue moon." Marcia continued. "When I agreed to take this case, Jerry filled me in on the preliminaries of his wife's case and gave me some initial information about what kind of woman she is. She takes her religion seriously and that's what's making this so hard on her. Killing someone is one of the commandments, isn't it? I mean, not killing anyone. Oh, you know what I mean."

"Anyhow, she's admitted to wanting to hit her kids, especially lately," Marcia added, "but she's justifiably angry with them. After all, they've given those kids a good, stable home but they've chosen to live like others who come from broken homes or no homes at all. As far as I know she's never hit them in anger but the children complain they can never talk to their parents and their mother is always "mad" at them, to use their words."

"As far as I know she's a caring Mother," said Marcia, "and a good wife although she does tend to dominate. I intend to interview some of her friends even though I don't think she has too many. That's strange too, because you would think that with her church involvement for all these years, there would be more people whom she would be close to." Marcia knew she was reaching but she knew so little about this woman who was her client. She hadn't known how little until Mary asked her these questions.

Mary hesitated for a few minutes and then proceeded to tell Marcia about another client of hers that was serving time for manslaughter. "This woman came from a seemingly normal lifestyle, at least normal in the Christian sense. One day, she was walking across a parking lot towards her favorite clothing store when she picked up a rock and hurled it through the window of the store. As you can imagine, shards of glass exploded into the store and a customer was killed. Afterwards, she couldn't even remember picking up the stone but others saw her do it. She's serving five years at Pemlico."

"That's exactly what my client says happened to her. She can't remember doing any of the things they said she did." Marcia was getting excited. Maybe this Mary could help Debra after all.

Mary continued. "My client had been abused for years by her husband and even though they lived and breathed their church involvement, no one ever knew. She always felt that the church teachings sanctified her husband's treatment of her and in fact he would misquote the scriptures all the time in defense of his beatings."

Mary began to display anger herself when she added, "He wasn't just mildly involved in the church either. He was an Elder! That's supposed to be a privilege reserved for men who have their households in order and they are the ultimate leaders of the church. In a lot of cases, these men interpret scripture to mean controlling their wives whereas the Bible says they are to love their wives as Christ loved the church, His bride."

"Each incident of abuse toward my client produced an anger inside her that was finally triggered that day in the parking lot" she said. "It had become so great that she lost control and became almost literally blinded by it. When people do not deal with their anger but keep stuffing it inside themselves, one day something simple and altogether unrelated will trigger it and then watch out."

"You mean, like the battered wife syndrome? I saw that movie on TV with, what's her name in it? Lindsay Wagner or was it Farah Fawcett? Anyway, she was the one who set her husband's bed on fire. Like that?" Marcia snapped her fingers. She was really trying hard to understand what Mary was saying. After all, her defense strategy could come from this angle.

"It's something like that," Mary continued, "only, in this case it just happens out of the blue. The person has no idea what to expect or what they're doing; it's so intense an anger. It's like the straw that broke the camel's back scenario. If your client experienced something like this then there is probably some abuse somewhere in her life that she's not dealt with. I would like to see her and explore this a little further. Do you think you can talk her into coming in?"

"I'll try but are you covered by insurance?" Marcia asked. "I'm not sure of their financial status and I know they will have to extend themselves a long ways to pay for this trial coming up. I'll ask them to see if they want to pursue this angle but I think it's a good bet."

Standing, Marcia held out her hand to Mary as the latter said, "Their church may have a program in place that offers free counseling for so many visits. Ask them to check it out. Otherwise we aren't covered by the usual plans. Good Luck. I hope you can help your client."

They shook hands and after thanking Mary, Marcia left to discuss setting up some appointments with Mary with her client. She felt that even if the counseling didn't help her client's case, it could certainly help her client.

The morning was turning into a bright sunny one again. The traffic was getting heavier the closer Marcia drove toward the courthouse and the jail that incarcerated Debra. She knew that outside appointments would have to require a police escort but usually the police were willing to take someone if it involved their health. Marcia believed that counseling did indeed involve her client's health and well-being.

When she pulled into the parking lot for the third time in two days, Marcia couldn't help but notice the number of people holding hands. What was this, a lover's lane all of a sudden? Oh right, this is the courthouse. Those people had probably come here to get married by the judge. "If I ever get married," she thought, "It won't be by a justice of the peace. I want a big church wedding with a white dress, a long train and…How did I ever get on that train of thought?"

For a person who was pretty happy with her life, all of a sudden Marcia found many things to feel sorry about. Everywhere she looked, people were in couples. Did couples rule the world? When had living alone become such a bad thing? "Get yourself together lady," she groused inwardly and marched boldly towards the main doors and into the courthouse. She followed yesterday's path to the elevator, and stood in front of the desk of the sergeant wielding the power to let her see her client or not.

"I need to see Debra Wiebe. I'm her lawyer," began the petite brunette who had, unbeknownst to her, become the topic of conversation for a group of officers standing near a water cooler at the back of the room.

"Who is she?" asked one lone uniformed officer.

"Jacobs, she's too high class for you," chided another male in plain clothes. "Now as for me…"

"Yah, right Sloan. What makes you better than me?"

"Women love a man who is in authority over them. And since I am the arresting officer for her client, I hold the key to her heart."

"Yes, but I'm eligible and you're not," struck Officer Jacobs. "Besides, I think her client will win this case. She was clearly not in her right mind when I arrived at the scene."

"Yah, well, I aim to prove that she knew that guy and that her intentions were premeditated," snipped Sloan, a big burly cop with an attitude. "I plan to put that dame on ice for a long time."

"Well, I saw her. She was not coherent and if that lawyer calls me for the defense, I plan to say just that."

"Oh what do you know? You're just a rookie," slammed Sloan. "You're still wet behind the ears and obviously a poor judge of character if you think that woman is innocent."

Unaware of their scrutiny and their conversation, Marcia followed the desk sergeant towards the back of the room and a doorway leading to the jail. Inside, another officer, a jailor this time, took her into the interrogation room closest to the cellblock and went to find her client.

"Wiebe, your lawyer's here again. Boy, she must be preparing some defense. Too bad it won't work and you'll be spending a long time behind these bars," he sneered. "Someone who'd kill in cold blood like that deserves to hang, if ya ask me."

"Ah whatta you know?" Suzette retorted with a loud clang of her cup on the bars. "Leave the woman alone, will ya? Go get em, hon," she added for Debra's benefit.

Debra was marched into that small room once again to face more questions from a woman she had just met such a short while ago. Marcia's questions were always so personal and today Debra was not in the mood to answer anyone anything ever again.

"Now what," she began. "More stupid questions again?"

Marcia blinked. She certainly never expected her client to kiss her on the cheek when she came for a visit but she was not prepared for this anger nor the force with which it

85

was delivered toward her. What did Debra think, that she could just defend her without any help from her client?

"Sit, and let's get started. First off, put that temper on hold. We have a lot of work to do and no time for one of your tantrums." For a small frame Marcia could deliver a solid punch with a bunch of words. Debra sat.

"I hate this place and the guards are positive I will lose. They keep talking about my long stay in here or hanging me. Can they do that?"

"Not in this state. Besides, they don't know what they are talking about. Are you willing to sit with a Christian counselor to figure out why you are so angry all the time?"

"What do you mean, all the time? Whom have you been listening to?"

"Your kids," said Marcia.

"Oh." Debra hung her head. She knew she had been angry more days than not lately and that the two living at home did not deserve a mother such as she had been to them. They were good kids and should have a home where they didn't have to walk on eggshells around their mother.

"Okay, set up the appointments. But how can I keep outside appointments from here?"

"The police will escort you to them, as many as you need. The number will depend on your therapist."

"At least I'll get to be free for a couple of hours each time then. When will they start?" Debra had calmed down some but Marcia could see that her emotions were still very ragged. Things outside her control seemed to set her off. Interesting!

"I'll set up your first appointment as soon as you get back from the hospital. Now try to stay calm and think about anything else that might help explain why you killed that boy the other day. I'll see you tomorrow at the hospital to let you know what I've found out. Today I plan to begin questioning everyone I can who knows you."

Debra was returned to her cell and, drained from her earlier outburst, she lay on her bed and closed her eyes. Life was not fair, she thought as she drifted off into a fitful sleep.

CHAPTER SEVEN

In what seemed like only minutes, the same guard who had escorted her earlier awakened Debra. "Wake up Wiebe," he shouted at her. "You're off ta tha looney bin."

"Okay, just give me a minute to gather my stuff," Debra replied groggily. She gathered up her Bible that Jerry had brought for her and the two study guides he had also brought, studies she had been working on at home. She made sure to take everything else that he and the kids had purchased for her since she didn't know what she would be allowed to have at the hospital.

The guard opened her cell door and they walked down the hall. She was not going to miss this place, she thought but then she also thought about her new friend. "Sa ya," Suzette hollered.

"Yah, see ya," answered Debra as the guard shouted at the two of them to be quiet.

Once outside, Debra was escorted toward a police car sitting by the side of the street with it's motor running. As they approached so did the two officers who would make the ride with her, one of them a female.

"I don't think we'll need handcuffs this time," said Jacobs. "Will we Mrs. Wiebe?"

"No, I'll be okay. You're the officer from the scene of the accident aren't you?"

"Yah right...Some accident," interrupted the female officer. "Get in the back seat and let's get this show on the road." She was clearly in charge so Debra complied as quickly as she could. "You keep to yourself back here and we'll get along just fine," the officer added.

Debra drank in the sunlight shining on all the glass windows of the buildings located in this area of town. She watched people walking to and from their workplace and the other pedestrians obviously looking for a bargain or maybe going to lunch with someone. Freedom...would she ever feel it again?

The car moved forward through traffic and made it's way toward the edge of town. Before long they were driving in the country and Debra noticed the colors as she had never before. It's funny how we take so much of God's creation for granted when we have it available to us every day, she thought.

The drive took them into a part of the country she hadn't been in a long time. Debra noticed many changes but she also noticed that the farmhouses seemed shabbier and that the fields were not as weed free as they had been the last time she had traveled this road. I guess it tells us that the economy here is not too great, she surmised.

A short half hour later, they had reached a large brick structure with several other buildings around it. Officer Jacobs pulled the police car up to the front door and turned off the engine. They piled out and with Debra between them, they marched up the steps to the front door. Opening the huge glass door, they entered a large hollow sounding foyer where a receptionist greeted them.

"May I help you," she asked.

Jacobs handed her some paperwork, a sheaf of forms that he had taken from the front seat of the car. He waited while she perused the documents and then she called someone on the intercom.

A tall man, who appeared to be in his mid-thirties, walked smartly towards them from one of the offices located nearby. He held out his hand to Debra and said, "Hi, I'm Dr Fry. I'll be working with you over the next few weeks to make the determination that the courts need. Welcome to Clarkville."

Debra couldn't help but respond to his kind manner and slow smile. She took his hand and the doctor led her away from the police officers who then turned and left the building the way they had come. She was once again in the hands of strangers but at least she felt that this one was a kind person.

"Why don't we sit in here for a little while and get acquainted, shall we?" said Dr. Fry. With that he opened a door and ushered Debra into a small room that was furnished with comfortable sofas and chairs usually seen in people's living rooms. "Take a seat Debra and let's get started."

"First off, would you like some coffee? Was the drive out a pleasant one? How do you take it?" he said as he poured a cup for each of them.

"I take it black and yes it was a nice drive. It was good to be out of jail even if I was in a police car with two officers."

"Well, what we will try to do here is find out if you are competent to stand trial. I haven't read anything about your case yet so right now let's just get to know each other a little better. I will be the one you will see most of the time although others on staff will be doing some of the testing we will need for a fair evaluation. How are you feeling, today?"

"I'm feeling fine except for the fact that I've appeared to have killed someone."

"Does that bother you?"

"Of course it does," she answered quickly. "I never met the man before in my life and the police are going to try to prove that I did it deliberately because I hated him or something." Debra's voice held an edge to it that Dr. Jonathan Fry had heard a number of times with patient's who had a problem controlling their anger.

"We'll get into all that in due course. For now let's just enjoy a pleasant visit, shall we?" he said in that psychiatric voice Debra believed all doctors who treated insane people had.

"I'm not insane Dr. Fry," she said with equal calm in her voice, "but I do get angry more often than I would like."

"We'll see if we can fix that too," he replied. "Now tell me about yourself. Are you married?"

"Yes Jerry and I have been married for 22 years. Will he be able to come often to visit?" Debra clung to the thought of her husband and his support for her in this awful situation. "He brought me all this stuff in jail. Can I put it somewhere?"

"Of course. Why don't I get a basket from the receptionist office for you to carry all that stuff a little easier? I see you have a Bible with you. Do you read it often?"

"Yes, every day. Is that okay in here? I don't know all your rules yet."

"You can read that book whenever you want as well as any books you want to take out of our library. In this hospital, you will have the freedom to move about your ward anytime you want and you can go to the coffee shop, library, or recreation facility with a pass that the staff on your wards will provide once you are all settled in. Your meals will be taken with other patients in a large cafeteria and, I might add, they are pretty tasty. Now let's get back to you. Do you have any children?"

"Yes, we have four. The oldest is 20 and the youngest is six. We have three boys first and then our little girl is the six year old. The oldest two are living in an apartment in town, though.'

"Do you live in a house?" continued Dr. Fry. The questions he asked were very general in nature as he tried to draw Debra out, helping her to feel comfortable with her new accommodations. They visited for another half hour and then Dr. Fry said, "I think it's time for you to get settled in. Dinner will be ready shortly. What do you think?"

"I'm ready. I'm tired and I quess…a little hungry," said Debra as she once again prepared to gather her belongings in her arms.

"Oh right," said Dr. Fry. "I said I would get you a basket. Let's go back to reception for that on our way to your ward."

As they left the room and started walking back through the foyer to the other end of the large airy room, Dr. Fry added, "I think you will like the accommodations we have for you. It's not like a hotel but we try to make our patients as comfortable as possible."

"Thank you," Debra said in a rather timid voice considering they had been talking for so long already.

"Debra does this place intimidate you?"

"I-I guess it does a little." She replied. "I miss Jerry, too."

"Well we'll see what we can do to get him to visit tomorrow, shall we. In the meantime, let's go meet some of the other staff especially the ones you will be working with directly."

Dr. Fry took her back again the way they had just come towards a door located on the opposite wall from the entry. He pressed a buzzer and the door automatically opened. "This door is locked every night but during the day, when our patients have visitors or need to come to this area of the building, it is unlocked. However, to get here, you will need a pass," explained the kind voice.

Debra followed him down a long hallway with doors marked as administrative offices of one kind or another. There were lots of doors she noticed. They stopped in front of an elevator then and Dr. Fry pressed the up button. The doors opened and they entered a comfortable looking little room with a bench located along the back wall. "Sometimes our patient's have to be medicated and it's just easier if they have a place to sit while in the elevator," he said.

It was a short ride to the floor Dr. Fry had pushed. The elevator door opened and the sight that met them surprised Debra. This section of the hospital looked just like a large home with several rooms located off one main room that was furnished with some of the same patterned sofas and chairs as the small visitor's room they had used earlier. Two colorfully attired people left a room that looked as if it might be an office to greet them when they entered.

"Dr. Fry, Mrs. Wiebe, we have been expecting you," one of them said with a smile and a handshake.

"Debra, this is Jane Carlson and that is Barbara Wooton. They are on staff here as psychiatric nurses and work with our patients to make sure that everything is looked after. They will get you to your appointments with me as well as appointments with all the other people who will be working with you. Jane, Barbara, this is Debra. Will you show her the room you have picked out for her?"

"Certainly doctor. Come Debra, let's get you settled in." And with that, the pair led her towards a room just to the right of the office and Dr. Fry left them to get acquainted. "We have only four other people living in this ward at the moment so its not too crowded," said Barbara as they opened the door to the brightest room Debra had ever seen. The walls were yellow with yellow flowered curtains on the large picture window. The bedspread on what appeared to be a queen sized bed matched the curtains. Two easy chairs, a small writing desk and a large dresser completed the room's décor. The room was the largest bedroom Debra had ever seen except on TV.

"Oh-h-h, this is pretty," she exclaimed as she put her basket of stuff on the bed. "Will I have to wear this awful jumpsuit here all the time? They didn't bring me any other ones to change into."

"No, check out that closet," said Jane. Inside the only other door in the room was a large closet area with another door leading to a bathroom, also decorated in yellows. The closet had about five different combinations of pants and pullover shirts, which looked to be just the right size. They were similar to the ones worn by the nurses.

"How can you tell the patients from the nurses here?" she laughed for the first time since arriving.

"Oh we have our ways," the two nurses spoke in unison. "Why not take a nice hot shower, change into some clean clothes. And by the way, everything else you will need is in

97

that dresser over there. Then we will show you where you can get something to eat. Tomorrow morning we will go over your schedule."

Debra looked around her and began to feel very much at home. She smiled her thanks as the two nurses left and closed the door behind them. She began to peel the zipper of her jumpsuit down as she moved into the bathroom and a nice, long, hot, soapy shower. Oh, to feel fresh and clean again, she thought as she turned on the water.

CHAPTER EIGHT

Over the next week, Marcia talked to relatives, neighbors, and friends as well as Debra's pastor. The people from the church knew her rather well. She discovered that Debra was born in a small town in the northern part of one of the eastern states. Along with her seven siblings-three brothers and four sisters-they were a close-knit family; but her family was now scattered all over the country. Most of them she only saw once in two years, and they were not the same anymore.

Each had gone separate ways and had found their own way to a settled, if not especially happy, life. Happiness to each of them meant something different but to Debra the road had led to the church and her Christian faith. Her siblings and most of their children did not understand the convictions of her family but they never allowed it to complicate their once in a while family gathering.

As a small child, Debra remembered happy times with her family, mostly her brothers and sisters. Fun was something she couldn't equate with her parents. As children, they used to play house in an old delivery van that sat at the back of their house or pretend to be explorers in the bush growing nearby. To this day she doesn't know how big the "bush" was or if it was even safe but they had fun there anyway.

"Skunk Hollow" was the name they gave their discovery, when one day they found a small canyon deep in the forest containing small holes or burrows all up and down its sides. This was their box canyon where they would capture wild horses, campout for pretend nights, or escape from the sheriff's posse. Their imagination knew no bounds as they enacted scenes from the new TV set their father had just purchased.

They would take their cousins on trips of exploration and laugh with glee when these city slickers touched the wrong leaves and ended up with a rash for weeks. She often wondered in later years whether her parents ever worried about them, for she knew she could never allow her own children to wonder so far from home for so long.

Debra was by every classification, a tomboy. Climbing trees, climbing into haylofts, and catching snakes to hurl into trees, were all activities of her childhood. She liked nothing better than to don a pair of jeans or old pants and play outside with the boys. Whenever they played house in the old van, she was the daddy unless they could talk one of the boys into playing with them. She used to love to visit an aunt who lived on a farm in the hill country. There she could explore new places and meet new people. Her aunt never watched out for her either or if there were any restrictions they were not noticeable.

She could climb into the hayloft and look for miles into the valley never thinking of the danger that lay at her feet. On one of these climbing adventures, she fell many feet to the ground below just missing a large rock with her head. Climbing became something one only pursued in an emergency after that and her feeling of dizziness, when confronted with high places, persisted to this day.

Debra loved animals and their family always had a dog. Their house was built over a cellar that they could access from the outside. One day while roaming the yard with Buster, the family dog, she discovered an animal trapped under the stairs leading to their back door. It looked to her like a cute, cuddly, brown animal and she couldn't stand to see him in distress.

Without thinking she used a stick to try to help him to escape, but this animal was so scared that it only bit the stick in two. Gradually by pushing on the boards holding him, she managed to allow him to back out but by that time her father was there. He told her it was a groundhog and that it would bite her.

The animal escaped to their cellar and her father chased the dog after it to catch it. She was devastated and cried for hours after Buster caught the groundhog and broke its back with one shake of his head.

She could not understand this cruel side to her father but she knew his temper was always close to the surface so she never talked to him about this. Her tears were shed in private in an outbuilding used for storing yard maintenance equipment. She was even angry at her dog but she knew he didn't know any better.

Debra's relationship with her mother was strange in those days. It always appeared to Debra that her mother was forever working since playing was not something grownups seemed to do. Cooking meals, mending clothes, washing clothes, ironing clothes, sweeping floors, washing floors-the list was endless. The children were never expected to help out so all day was play for them but their mother was always in the background of their lives.

She was the one who made sure they developed habits of cleanliness and the Saturday night bath ritual before the oil-burning stove was a fond memory. All of them, using the same bath water heated over a wood burning stove and contained in a galvanized tub, would be scrubbed clean for the week to come. Their hair was washed and always there were clean pajamas to put on afterwards warmed by the oil stove. They had two stoves, one for heating (the oil stove) and one for cooking, the wood stove.

Her mother was a meticulous housekeeper making sure each tiny room in that house was always spotless. Even the outhouse was cleaned regularly to avoid spider webs when one sat down. She appeared older to her children as do most parents to their children but she had the ability to work such long hours so her health was always good. They never thought of her getting sick and in fact, seemed to take her for granted most of the time.

Her father was another matter entirely. He was the one who disciplined and usually with lots of anger. He wanted his children to be obedient, eat all their vegetables, tie their own shoelaces before going to grade one, take his side over their mother's in an argument, and above all else never question him on anything.

He was the only authority they were to listen to and although he sent them to school, he always knew better than the teachers. Anything they learned was hogwash if he didn't understand it. His 4th grade education left him knowing very little about the world but he always had an opinion and it was always the right one.

Overshadowing their fun times, were the bouts of drinking and the ensuing angry tirades that left them all scared to breathe. They knew that if their father was not around for a couple of days, he would be home soon and they would have to tread lightly for another couple of days.

He loved their dog, or so they thought. However, one day when a neighbor's Chihuahua came into their yard, Buster who was much larger, decided to fight with it. Debra's father grabbed their dog and threw him up against a tree breaking two of his ribs. He liked the Chihuahua better they deduced and decided his love for them was probably as fickle.

School was an opportunity to develop friendships outside her family and Debra loved going there. The school she attended was located a fair distance from home so when she left on the school bus in the morning, she was gone all day. She was picked up at the end of the driveway before eight each morning and deposited back at 4 o'clock every afternoon. The school bus was an old beat-up yellow contraption driven by an older man of immense proportions. He was easy to obey for he loved the children he drove each day and they knew it.

Those days, no one heard of child abductions or molestation's so their world was considerably safer than the one children of today live in. The teachers at school were very strict but fair and Debra's grades were always good. She had three best friends at school who all lived in different areas but they went everywhere together during their school day. Two of them lived close enough to the school to go home for lunch while she and the other girl brought their lunch to school.

She never knew that her clothes were shabbier than her friends or that their houses were in better condition than hers. It seemed not to matter and so was never discussed.

An incident that sticks out in her mind during the fifth grade was her first love letter from a boy in her class. She found it hidden in a pocket of her desk when she arrived that morning but forgot it there when the teacher asked her to change desks with another boy. That boy found it and proceeded to read it. The teacher caught him and read the note in front of the whole class. It was extremely embarrassing at the time but became a warm memory deep in her heart. She felt pretty for the first time even though that boy never talked to her after that uncomfortable day. She learned that there were nice boys and there were not so nice boys who teased and made her feel foolish.

Another school memory was of one particular teacher who seemed to have faith in her no matter what. She was strict but appreciated a good effort and applauded work well done. Mrs. Farris was also a Sunday school teacher and for a couple of years, Debra was allowed to walk the mile or so to the small country church where she learned for the first time all about Jesus. These were stories she loved to hear over and over again and so never turned down the chance to attend Vacation Bible School during the summer or the Christmas concerts. Her parents would attend at Christmas time and she would perform her lines with pride hoping to please them and show them the things she had learned.

Summer time always brought a time of boredom interspersed by a trip to visit an Aunt in a nearby town on a Sunday afternoon or a trip to the beach not far from them. On these trips, her father would sing from the driver's seat and the children would join in on the words they knew. They would be given a dime or a nickel to spend at the store their relatives operated or to spend at the beach concession stand.

They felt so rich when they were allowed to spend the money on anything they liked. The beach was the best fun, for it was at these times that all the relatives would gather for picnics and their father would play with them a little in the water. Debra loved the water and even though she didn't know how to swim, she could push people off the floating dock with the best of them and she could dog paddle her way to safety whenever she was pushed in.

Adolescence brought some new responsibility and more anger from her Dad. He was always accusing her of something and using words she had to look up in the dictionary. The boys in her neighborhood teased her and the game "robin hood"-a game during which the boys would chase the girls, tackle them and then snap the back of their bra-was their favorite pastime. By now, they lived in a more populated area where their circle of playmates was much broader but they had to change schools. She lost track of her three best friends and so she tried to acquire new ones, something that never really happened ever again. It seemed that no matter whom she chose, they were not good enough for her father and he would use names like "Slut and Whore "to describe who she was becoming.

Wearing any kind of makeup, or talking to a boy in broad daylight would bring on one of these verbal attacks. Debra became more introverted the older she got. She knew her parents didn't like her and so her first thoughts of living on her own would materialize in fantasy form, as she would sit under a leafy shade tree to think.

She loved to read and would often be found with her head in a book especially at the new school where she did know she was not as well off as her contemporaries. Even though they wore uniforms most of the time, the once or twice a month they didn't was very painful. During those early teenage years, she learned that not all fathers got drunk, and that a lot of people owned their own homes. They were renters and everyone seemed to know it.

The rest of the years, living in her parent's house until she was sixteen years of age, could be classified as full of turmoil. The words anger, fighting, skipping school, falling grades, hand-me-down clothes, sneaking out to have a boyfriend and unfair restrictions all described her last years at school. She managed to complete the 12th grade but not with the marks her parents knew she was capable of. She was never allowed to join any of the after school clubs so never made a lot of friends.

Loneliness and shyness were her constant companions and she looked forward to having a full time job so she could help out at home and have some clothes of her very own. When her father discovered her plans did not include university, his hostility forced her out on her own. At first she was devastated for he only gave her 24 hours to make the move but very quickly she began to enjoy her new freedom.

She had a good job where she got along with everyone and her second roommate was a very caring, young, married woman who patiently taught her to socialize in a lady-like manner. Some things were fast eye-openers. Her boyfriend at the time proved untrustworthy and her first roommate turned out to be a prostitute but she learned expeditiously.

Debra discovered she preferred older boys, or almost men to boys her own age and she could behave in a very grown-up, sophisticated manner. She loved clothes and her dates during the next two years were marked by excuses for new outfits to accompany her current date. She welcomed lots of dates and chose to be charming, witty, and fun to be with…within limits. Self-improvement was her goal. She learned whatever it took to remove her high school stigma of "plain Jane" and "carpenter's dream".

By the time she was eighteen and a half, she was engaged and had moved to the west where her fiancé became her nucleus. For two years or more, she did most things to please him forgetting her goals of self-improvement and because he was so much a part of her life, her circle of friends disappeared. Even the friend who had moved with her, slid into the background of her life. Her fiancé's demands on her escalated and after drinking too much one night, he raped her.

She had no one to turn to and even though she arrived home in tatters, bruised about her arms and face, no one believed her. Two weeks later, loneliness dictated her forgiveness of him and their relationship progressed in the way he had wanted all along. Fortunately he was living and working out of town, so she was only subjected to his advances once or twice a month.

Six months later, Debra was faced with a dilemma that would change her life once more when she discovered she was pregnant. She was terrified after her fiancé broke their engagement even though she knew by this time it wasn't love she felt for him. Suicide seemed her only answer but she discovered she had strength within her to survive even this. Her days were difficult and lonely but she gave birth to a baby girl and then felt the heartbreak of separation as she placed her for adoption.

Debra was 20 years old and felt like thirty for a long time after that. Anyone she met seemed too young for her and she felt like she had a mark on her forehead telling everyone far and wide what kind of person she was.

Marriage was in the cards for her though, for by the time she was 22, she had met a wonderful man, who, throughout their almost two years of dating, taught her many things, as he also learned from her. After marriage, they had their arguments and although it took her a long time to believe him, when he said, "till death do us part", he meant it. He taught her a lot about commitment.

They gave birth to four children and life seemed to be kind of wonderful to her for a long time. She worried from time to time about her lost baby, but she became so preoccupied with her family that the times of sorrow shortened and she accepted her decision.

During the early years of her marriage she met, for the first time, the person of Jesus Christ in a personal way and learned all He had done for her. He became real to her and her personal faith took on meaning. Her church attendance to that point had been non-existent, as had her husband's as long as she had known him but now she was eager to go and have these wonderful principles instilled in her children's life.

There were a couple of years of solitary church attendance but then Jerry joined her and they became an even closer family. She taught her children biblical reasons for the rules that were necessary to make them Godly people and developed methods of discipline that would ensure she would not treat them as harshly as she had been raised. She told them often how much she loved them, and if she was not as demonstrative as she should have been, her husband was.

He read to them each night and said their prayers with them as he tucked them in. There were spankings but there was also lots of fun and they played together as a family whenever they could. Trips during their summers made for fond memories and they carried their faith with them wherever they went. For twelve years they worked hard in the church and Debra's self-esteem seemed strong and high.

Then, their boat was rocked, leaving them needing to make choices not before thought about. Her lost daughter sent a letter wishing to see her after an eighteen-year separation. Debra had always worried about her getting sick and dying or being abused by her adoptive parents, so now she would be able to find out if her decision of all those years ago was the right one.

However, no one in her family except her husband knew of her past and no one in the church did either. Even her children had, until now, been too young for her to tell although she had planned on telling them someday about their older sister. All went smoothly though and she was reunited during a very tearful meeting. Her children seemed very accepting and she learned to overlook anyone who was not, as far as her church family went. Forgiving herself was part of her learning process during those days and she felt she had succeeded.

Life took on another dimension now as she tried to juggle her time with her daughter and her family but quickly things settled down. She was able to step back from her first born to allow her daughter's own family their place. She had no more questions about her long ago decision and her life moved on. Her children were growing up and their adolescence, so far, was going smoothly.

Suddenly, though, all that changed as her two oldest children started doing things Debra and her husband had only read about. Rebellion with a capital "R" filled their home and life became a battleground as these two Christian parents tried to keep their offspring from destroying their lives and the lives of their younger siblings.

Each incident caused them to question their faith at first but as much as they could understand, they tried to place their children in God's hands and not worry. Painful, sleepless nights became the norm and after a long time all they could do was use these times to pray for their children. Eventually the two moved out at an age much younger than either of their parents had anticipated but things at home became quieter after that. As parents they were able to separate their youngest two from the pain they were feeling for their older two, so life once again became somewhat peaceful or so it seemed until now.

CHAPTER NINE

It took Marcia almost another full week to compile all the information that she hoped would give her some idea as to why her client might have done what she did. As she perused Debra's file, however, she puzzled over the lack of any clue that would lead her to understand the motives of her client. Debra's life seemed so normal that there was nothing to indicate why she had murdered that man. The abuse that Mary, from that counseling center, had been looking for seemed to be nonexistent. In fact Debra's life was almost dull compared to the clients that Marcia usually acquired.

She decided to see if Jonathan Fry still worked at the Clarkville Psychiatric Facility before she made a visit to her client. Phone calls had been okay but she needed to touch base with Debra and go over some of the material she had gathered.

Jonathan's opinion, if he was still at the facility, might help her decide a different course of action if that was what was needed to free Debra and maybe that Christian place was out to lunch anyway. Jonathan would probably be able to evaluate the situation by now and maybe shed some light on the reasons behind the deed.

As she dialed, Marcia remembered the last time she had talked with him. As much as they had tried hard to maintain their friendship after Jonathan was married, they had lost track of one another and she'd not seen him in a couple of years.

"May I speak with Dr, Jonathan Fry, please?" she responded when her call was answered.

"Dr. Fry is in a meeting right now. Would you like to leave a message?" came the proficient answer on the other end of the line.

"No but could I make an appointment to see him as soon as possible?"

"Would tomorrow morning be too soon?"

"No that would be great. I have to come visit a client anyway. What time do you have open?"

"Dr Fry's schedule for the morning is pretty flexible. How about 9 a.m?" the receptionist said.

"That'll work. Thank you." said Marcia as she hung up. Her mind reflected on the man she had known for some time. "Jonathan Fry—ummmm," she thought to herself. The last time she had seen him, he spent the whole time bragging about his wife. She wondered if he was still as happy in his marriage. Her thought that Jonathan was a nice man and deserved to be happy placed an end to that train of thought as Marcia put on her coat and decided to call it a day. Tomorrow she would continue her hunt in defense of her client.

Leaving about 8 a.m. the next morning, the drive to the center took her over half an hour but the countryside was beautiful. Marcia didn't get the opportunity to drive in unfettered surroundings very often and if it hadn't been such a long day ahead of her, she would have taken more time to thoroughly enjoy it. After a couple of weeks fact gathering, there was still so much more she needed for the profile on her client.

When she had talked to her on the phone to discuss her life, Debra had not been an easy person from whom to glean information. There were so many details that she felt were unimportant and she was a woman who didn't easily talk about life. Eighty percent of anything Marcia had learned had appeared by a question and answer interrogation method that made her feel as if she were pulling teeth. That was hard work and after all this time, she seemed to be no closer to learning the truth of her client's case than she was when she had started. "This trip today had better change all that," she thought.

Jonathan was her last hope to discovering why a seemingly normal woman would do what Debra had done and then have no memory of it. There was always the outside chance that Debra was faking the memory loss but even that scenario didn't fit this woman's profile. She seemed honestly distraught that she could have done such a deed and more so, that she couldn't remember it.

As she entered the outskirts of Clarkville, Debra noticed that it was a small town. When she had looked it up on the map and then researched the website, she discovered that the town seemed mostly populated by the employees of the psychiatric center and their families. A convenience store and a gas station were the only other sources of employment in the area.

They had their local police force but that was relatively small. The tree lined approach to the center contained chattering birds of all kinds, native to the area and several places where flowerbeds had transformed the landscape with color and fragrance. The center itself was a large gray brick building with several small cottages surrounding the main edifice as well as larger out buildings. Clarkville had the reputation of being the most up-to-date facility in the country with several doctors on staff who had written papers on the effects of abuse as well as socio, economic, and environmental impact studies on the developing child.

Dr. Jonathan Fry had been one of the leaders in his field of research and used to lecture all over the country. Marcia was not too sure that he would be able to clear up this mystery but she knew that he would give it a good try. He had always told her that the work of a psychiatrist was like that of a detective sometimes. He dug around in his patient's head for facts starting with one tiny glimmer. The true curiosity seeker was taken vociferously further in his search to bring other facts to surface. Most of the important clues the patients themselves didn't even know existed and so his knowledgeable probing would develop into the facts needed.

Parking her car and then getting out, Marcia stretched her legs and then her back. She had been so eager to finish the profile on Debra that she had skipped her morning walk for the last two days and now she felt it. When she looked towards the door she noticed Jonathan waiting on the steps leading to the building she wanted to enter. This building also housed anyone needing protective lockup and although the windows had bars on them, they seemed not to be too intrusive into the overall peaceful surroundings.

Marcia waved to her longtime friend and smiled as she remembered their last encounter. He was always playing jokes on someone and she had been the unfortunate recipient of his last attempt at hilarity. Someday she would repay with a vengeance but today she wanted to concentrate on the task at hand.

"Marcia, it's so good to see you," greeted Jonathan with his hand outstretched for a handshake. "My curiosity was certainly aroused when I saw your name on my schedule this morning. Nothing wrong I hope?"

"No Jonathan. It's about a client who happens to be one of your patients," began Marcia as she took his hand. The pair of professionals walked into the building as Marcia explained Debra's situation and why she felt that it would take some other explanation than just premeditation. "Debra claims to have never known that man. I have also not been able to come up with any explanation about her incredible anger that morning and then to have no memory about the incident."

"First of all I have worked several times with Debra already and although she admits to having a problem with her temper, she is sane as far as I can tell at this point in our evaluation. There are two reasons for someone to lose a memory in the circumstances that you describe," Jonathan explained. "The first could be from a severe blow to the head and since that doesn't appear to be the case then I feel that the second reason is our best bet. Trauma can play out in many ways, one of them resulting in memory loss. What we need to do is find out the cause of the trauma and then we will know how to treat the amnesia."

"I'm looking forward to seeing her," Marcia said. "I really haven't discussed any of this with her yet. I just finished her profile, and she wants to visit with a Christian Family Counselor but since the puzzle is still there, I thought that I would just check this idea out with you first. I've never handled a case so full of contradictions before. She seems like such an upstanding citizen, one who has never been in any kind of trouble before and yet she appears to have deliberately killed a man she had neither met nor seen before."

"I want to discuss what I have found out so far with Debra and, can I tell her about your evaluation so far?" asked the lawyer. Marcia had a clear idea of what their defense would be but with so many pieces to the puzzle still missing, she needed a lot of time yet to make a clear evaluation herself.

"Are you planning on pleading innocent by reason of temporary insanity?" asked Jonathan. "It's clear to me, unless something unexpected happens between now and the end of Debra's one month here, that you won't be able to go for a straight insanity plea. There are certainly some circumstances that need clarifying. Not to change the subject but I have to go into the city next week sometime or maybe sooner. Can we get together to discuss this case some more?"

Jonathan walked Marcia through the clinic toward the elevators. The chimes on the clock in the foyer rang ten times when the door opened and she was ushered to the fifth floor where her client was living.

Jonathan walked into the room with her, introduced her to Barbara and Jane who were on duty together again and left to see to his other patients. "Call me," he said and was gone.

"Debra, you have a visitor," said Barbara when she knocked on the door to their patient's room.

"Come in," said Debra and as Marcia opened the door into the surprisingly cheerful room, Debra put the book down that she had been reading.

"My, isn't this the lap of luxury," Marcia remarked with a big grin on her face. "Debra it's good to see you face to face again. How have you been? You're looking good."

"I've been doing okay. This place and Dr. Fry are remarkable. They have given me all sorts of tests, the food is great, and I have a lot of freedom that, until I was incarcerated, I had taken for granted. Jerry comes at least three times a week and they even let him visit me in this room with the door locked," she said with a twinkle in her eye.

"Do you have your own bathroom?" Marcia asked.

"Sure, come see," Debra responded as she moved towards the one other door in the room. Marcia was once again pleasantly surprised at the accommodations for her client. "I certainly will not worry any more about how you are doing," she added. "Now let's get down to business. I have talked with the entire list of people you gave me. So far no one has given me any information that would shed any light on why this has happened to you. I think, once you are released from here, I will ask the judge to set your bail so we can get you home. Then we can pursue your visits to the counseling center."

"Do you think he will…the judge I mean…set my bail? It would be great to be home again. I miss the kids. Jerry has brought them here a couple of times but it's not the same."

"I think, no I am certain, that without any evidence that you knew the man who was killed, the judge will let you go home. The police have had a lot of time to find a tie but since we know they won't find one that directly ties you two together, the prosecution will have to agree."

"Oh…that sounds just heavenly," said Debra. "You've just made my day. What has Dr. Fry told you? Am I insane?"

"No, and you know you're not. He feels that at this point in your evaluation that you are definitely not insane and therefore are competent to stand trial. Which means that we have to alter our insanity plea to temporary insanity. That's harder to prove but I hope that the counselor at the Christian center will be able to help with that."

"Boy, I can hardly wait to begin in that case," added Debra.

"I'll see you in a week but if you ever need to talk to me you know how to get a hold of me," said Marcia, as she made ready to leave. "Take care and do everything the doctors tell you. How are you sleeping?"

"Like a baby. At first, they gave me some sleeping pills and for the first couple of days, I had a tranquilizer but now I don't need anything. I'll see you next week and thank you for all that you are doing. I don't know what I would do without you."

"It's just my job," said Marcia, at once knowing that she was going beyond just a job. She really liked this woman and planned to do her best, better than her best even.

"I know it's more than a job," said Debra, "and I am so grateful for your friendship. See ya."

Marcia retraced her steps to the elevator, and down to the first floor foyer. Jonathan was just saying good-bye to someone. When he saw her, he motioned for her to wait and walked with her out the door and into the midmorning sunshine.

"Thank you, Jonathan, for your time. By the way, how is your family these days?"

"I guess it has been awhile since we've seen each other," Jonathan replied with his head at an angle defeating his attitude of confidence. "My wife divorced me a year ago and although it was the best thing we've ever done for each other, I still feel such a failure at times. By the way, how is your client's relationship with her husband? He visits her here but since he isn't part of the evaluation, we don't talk to him at all. Sometimes a marital problem over a period of time could be a significant factor in the mental health of a person."

"As far as I know and from what I have observed, their relationship seems to be strong. Her husband is really supportive although he is rather baffled over her behavior. I'm sorry to hear about your marriage, Jonathan. I guess you have gotten over the initial grieving by now though."

Marcia had always had a soft spot for Jonathan. "Maybe we should get together for a drink when you come in next week!"

"That would be fun. I'll call you." Jonathan was quick on the uptake. Thinking about Marcia had once been a habit and he was looking forward to the possibility of renewing the practice. They had been friends ever since their college days.

Marcia waved as she pulled the car out of the parking lot. Turning towards the city, she engaged the cruise control and allowed her thoughts to drift to the next phase of her investigation or defense strategy. She needed to talk to Debra again and set up an appointment for her to see Jonathan and the woman at the counseling center as well. If temporary insanity was going to be their defense, Jonathan's testimony would be mandatory.

She also needed to talk to a mechanic. She wanted an impartial observer to go over every inch of that car to make sure it was not some mechanical failure that had caused the "accident". "Let's face it," she thought. "This case is one bizarre event and it's going to take a lot of work to get to the bottom of it."

The rest of Marcia's day consisted of a visit to another disgruntled client, arranging appointments at the Christian center for when Debra would be released, assuming that the judge would let her out on bail and seeking out the expert opinion of a mechanic. He told her that he would go over the car and arranged to have his tow truck pick up the car as soon as she could have it cleared. When she went to the impound yard at the police station to have the car released to the tow truck driver, she ran into Detective Sloan again and that sent her day into another spin.

"Howdy, Ms. Dixon," he began, his voice containing undertones of sarcasm. "I see you're still trying to find loopholes to get your client's charges dropped. Well that ain't gonna happen. I'm gonna nail that woman if it's the last thing I'll ever do."

"What makes you so determined Sloan? This can't be the only case you have to work on."

"No, not the only one but the only one that I intend to win no matter what. You didn't have to explain to the parents of that boy that their son was killed for no good reason and that the damage is so bad that they won't be able to even have an open casket. That woman murdered him and we intend to prove premeditation," the big detective growled. "You can wave your bleeding heart liberal attitude all over this place and it ain't gonna change the facts none."

"Sloan, my client did not know that man and you will not be able to prove otherwise," replied Marcia with a confidence she really didn't feel yet as she stalked off toward the impound office to seek out the man in charge.

Speaking of anger! Detective Sloan was almost taking this case personally. Maybe he was the one who knew the dead man before all this happened. Anyhow, he wasn't going to be able to prove his case, she told herself for the tenth time that day.

Once she had affected a release of Debra's car into the capable hands of the tow truck driver, Marcia left for her office. Several other clients needed her attention that day so her afternoon and early evening were spent looking after their needs. Just as she was thinking of leaving for the day, Jonathan called to say he would be in town the next day. "We can have that cup of coffee after that, if you'd like," he added.

"Sure Jonathan. What time can you be here?"

"How about two-ish?"

"Sounds good to me," she replied. "I'll see you tomorrow." Marcia hung up and then turned off all the lights in her office before closing and locking the door. She proceeded down the hall toward the elevator. Her office was located in the center of town, in one of the newest high rises with all the latest security gadgets so she was not worried about leaving the building on her own after dark. She left at this time of day so often that she really never gave it a second thought anymore.

It didn't take her long before she was on the street headed for home. The glaring lights from oncoming cars were hard on her eyes and by the time she pulled into her own driveway, she was relieved to be at home. It had been a long day but at least she was a little closer to knowing how her defense procedure would progress.

Locking up her car, her thoughts once again led her to her visit with Jonathan. She'd had a crush on him in college but he was involved already, with the woman who later became his wife. Maybe now that he was divorced, when they got together for that drink, something would evolve this time. She smiled at the prospect and discovered that she was looking forward to their meeting. Fumbling with her keys, she unlocked the door to her condominium. The future was something to look forward to after all!

CHAPTER TEN

The next day proceeded as normally as any of Marcia's days with plenty of paperwork and even some research for another client from the Internet. She was beginning to feel the need for a break when the intercom buzzed and her secretary told her that Dr. Fry was here to see her. "Let him in," she instructed as she cleared her desk to leave.

"Am I interrupting anything?" asked Jonathan as he entered the large spacious office that Marcia had furnished just a year ago when she had made partnership in the firm.

"No, I was just thinking that I needed to take a break. I've been working non-stop since eight this morning. Where would you like to go?"

"I don't know. You know the city better than I do. Why don't you pick a place?"

"Okay, I know just the spot. I'll drive. That way the country bumpkin won't get lost," she chided.

"Ho, country bumpkin eh? I'll show you," and they left amidst much laughter, something that until now, Marcia's secretary had only seen on rare occasions. She smiled, hoping that this man was a personal friend and not a would-be client. She enjoyed working for Marcia but felt that the woman worked too hard with little to keep her at home for someone so young.

Marcia and Jonathan kept up a steady stream of conversation all the way down in the elevator to the parking garage located in the basement of Marcia's building. They got in her car and proceeded to the street level where she turned north towards the El Paseo restaurant, a quaint ethnic establishment where cappuccino was served.

"Cappuccino, eh? I can remember when you didn't even drink coffee," said Jonathan.

"That was a long time ago. A person has to grow up sometimes."

"Well, so you think drinking coffee is a sign that a person is grown. What else marks a grown person?"

"Will you be serious for a change? I want to know what happened with your marriage. I thought it was so good," questioned Marcia. "Inquiring minds want to know, if that's not too personal, that is?"

"We just didn't get along anymore. I guess the straw that broke the camel's back though was when I found out she was seeing her old boyfriend behind my back. I would leave for work, she would leave for work or so I thought but she would actually go to her boyfriend's office. They would spend who knows how long together every day doing who knows what. This went on for almost a year before I caught on."

"I am so sorry," said Marcia. "I'll bet it hurt to find that out."

"Actually, we had grown so far apart by then that it was almost a relief to have it out in the open. She has moved in with him so I sincerely hope they are happy. As for me, I think I am finally ready to get on with my life...and right now I do not want to talk about that part any longer," he spoke with a teasing glint in his eye. "How come you've never married, Marce?'

"I just haven't found the right man, I guess. I've been pretty busy moving up the corporate ladder. I made partner last year so things have settled down a bit for me. Now when I have time, I have no one to spend it with. That's the way of the world though, don't you think? We strive for a certain goal thinking that it will make us happy and then when we get there, we discover we still aren't happy. But I am content…erck." She made a face by crossing her eyes with her tongue sticking out the side of her mouth. Here she was trying to convince a shrink that she was happy. Oh boy!

"Okay, I get the picture. Now how about we just get caught up and forget the entanglements in our life or, in your case, no entanglements?" Jonathan knew that with no obstacles, maybe this relationship could go places. He was glad they got all that out in the open.

"Thanks a lot! Rub it in, why don't you." Marcia grinned as she located a parking place near the restaurant and stopped the car.

"Let's try that delicious coffee you've been bragging about, shall we?" Jonathan said as he hopped out to open her door for her.

"Ummmm…Chivalry isn't a dead deal with Dr. Fry," she teased. "Thank you sir." They walked across the street and into a clearly Hispanic looking room with plenty of room for isolation if they wanted. Seclusion suited them to a tea so they chose a table off to one side and away from any current customers.

Marcia looked around, filled with a definite feeling of contentment. She hadn't been lying to Jonathan about feeling content with her life. If she hadn't worked so hard to get where she was, she wouldn't be in a position to help the Wiebe's. The money wasn't so bad either but it was helping people that made her most satisfied.

Jonathan felt the warmth of the atmosphere in this room and marveled at the similarities between he and Marcia. They had always liked the same things. When they were dating before, they could almost read each other's minds and now...they had a lot of catching up to do. He wanted to take things very slowly and make no promises. He wasn't about to get hurt a second time.

A waiter walked toward them with a menu but they both, at the same time, waved him away. "We just want some cappuccinos," she said. "Can you tell us what flavors you have?"

"I'll bring menu," he said in broken English.

"Jonathan, how long have you been working at Clarkville now. It's been quite a while, hasn't it?"

"Yes, about ten years. When I joined the staff there it was a full residential facility but now we do more out-patient care than residential. People like your client make up the bulk of our in-patient services. Courts are not as ready to accept an insanity plea without long-term evaluation. We see people anywhere from 30 to 90 days depending on how much work we have to do for the evaluation. There are so many facets to mental illness, that we try to be very thorough."

"In Debra's case, have you been thorough enough? Oh, I'm sorry. You're the professional psychiatrist here. Of course, you've been thorough."

"You mean, am I sure in my assessment after so short a time. When we get someone like Debra, with no prior history of violence, it's easy to assess. Whatever the reason behind her anger, we won't be able to tell with only one month but that's not what the courts are asking for. A person with an anger problem is not necessarily an insane person."

"But sane people don't go around mushing people against brick walls," added Marcia. "There has to be something causing that much anger."

"Oh I agree. It's just that I won't have enough time to get at the root in only a month. Since she is to be assessed for the court system, I can make that judgment in a month easy. The rest we'll have to deal with later. What do you think her chances are?"

"I plan to go back to court as soon as you've completed your evaluation and seek bail for her so she can return home. Then I have appointments all set up, once or twice a week with the Christian Counseling Center."

"That's a great idea. They do some good work especially in cases where a patient is a believer, as they say. They treat the whole person, body, soul, and spirit. I've worked alongside a couple of their people from time to time. Their methods are thorough, and you want thorough, right? And they seem to have no trouble making a person comfortable enough to talk. The institutional atmosphere here can be intimidating."

"I'm glad to hear you say that. I don't have any experience with them at all but I am sure hoping it works for Debra."

With their coffee ordered and a chance to talk like old times, the two became immersed in each other's life once again. He learned more about her than he had known in the past just by watching her as she talked about Debra. She found him easy to talk to, easier than her friend

Samantha in fact. Just as the coffee arrived, the doorbell over the door chimed and in walked the very person Marcia had just thought of.

Samantha was with another woman, maybe a client. But as soon as she walked through the door she noticed Marcia sitting there with a man, something that Marcia so seldom did. She couldn't help her curiosity, so being the out-going friendly sort, she sauntered over towards her friend.

"Hi Marcia, what's up?" she asked.

"Oh…nothing. Samantha I'd like you to meet Dr. Jonathan Fry, on staff at Clarkville. Jonathan, Samantha Benton. She used to be a friend of mine!"

"Used to be," interjected Samantha with a grin. "Hi, I'm pleased to meet you. Are you two working or can anyone join?"

"Ah-h-h…we're working," grinned Jonathan right back.

"Oh well then, I'll just let you two go back to woooork, if that's what's really going on. I'll talk to YOU later, Marcia," and with that Samantha walked smoothly over to her table and sat down.

140

"Darn," said Marcia. "Now she won't leave me alone until I tell her that we are sleeping together…errkk." and she made her famous face all over again.

Jonathan howled, something that just caused Samantha to stare all the more intently their way. Marcia knew that her friend, although with nothing but good intentions, was a romantic sort and could make a mountain out of a molehill. She didn't want Jonathan to feel any sort of pressure from her at all and she didn't relish any pressure about their relationship, should they get that far, either.

"Ah-h…where were we," she said.

"You were getting very red in the face, I think. Did you always blush so easy or is that something new?"

"I'd rather not talk about it, if you don't mind. I was enjoying our conversation before we were so rudely interrupted. Have you written any more books?"

"Okay, okay, I get the picture. Something neutral. Yes, I just finished a book on Alcohol and Drug Effects for Adolescents. It's about how they put their life and other lives in danger. I describe the cycles of depression and self-esteem as it relates to alcohol and drug abuse plus I added several chapters on breaking the law and getting arrested.

141

The book is intended for them to read about the effects of alcohol and drug abuse on schoolwork, their family, and their body and brain. There's a lot about the effects on their future, too."

"Oh, Jonathan that sounds really interesting, I didn't know you worked so closely with teenagers."

"I never used to but the numbers of teens being admitted to Clarkville by parents who can't handle their problems, or don't want to, has increased dramatically these past two years."

"I think that's interesting, I see them when they are caught and you're right, their numbers have increased lately. Teens used to think they were invincible. Now they just think that they will die anyway some day so why not do whatever they want now. It's a sad commentary on our world and the education system which can't seem to give these kids goals and purpose in life."

Marcia and Jonathan shared ideas about both their jobs for another hour before either noticed the time. When they did they were astounded to discover that the entire afternoon was gone and so was Samantha. Marcia never even noticed.

"Why don't we get a bite to eat seeing it's already that time of the day?" said Jonathan. "There's also a movie I've been meaning to watch. How about it? Wanna Come?"

"I am kind of hungry, come to think of it. What's the name of the movie?" And without giving it another thought, Jonathan and Marcia continued to visit. They ordered a delicious dinner, enjoyed a bottle of wine together and then left for the early show. The afternoon and evening were certainly shaping up, they both thought in unison.

CHAPTER ELEVEN

Over the next two weeks, Marcia worked hard for her client, talking frequently with the prosecutor who continued to be convinced that the police would be able to tie Debra to her victim. But so far, they hadn't and it was almost a month since the incident. Marcia was counting on their inability to do so when she scheduled another hearing before the judge to have Debra's bail set so she could go home. She had given Jerry a head's up about the amount it would probably be and he had been successful raising enough funds. Now it was simply a matter of getting Debra's evaluation done.

Jonathan continued to call her but they hadn't seen each other since that first time. And that was all right as far as Marcia was concerned. She had waited for the right man to come along for all these years so far; she could take her time and wait a little longer.

Jonathan had assured Marcia, however, that the evaluation would be ready and completed by this coming Friday, so Marcia set the court date for that afternoon. No point in having Debra spend any more time than necessary behind bars.

Marcia also spent some time with the mechanic who had Debra's car. He had stripped it down, almost to the frame, and still could not find any mechanical reason for the accident. At one point he even had the entire engine in pieces. "This is going to cost your client a pretty penny," he told Marcia when she phoned him two days ago. "I have checked this vehicle under a magnifying glass and if there is anything wrong, I certainly can't see it. Why in the world would your client carry all that perfume around with her? A bottle must have spilt and that stuff was so strong that I had to remove all the carpet and put it outside."

"As long as you save every piece of anything," said Marcia. "I may decide to get a second opinion. Not that I don't trust you but sometimes someone can find something that another person can't. You know, two heads are better than one."

"Oh, don't worry, since your client is facing a life sentence, I would expect you to be thorough. I saved everything and put the car back together just as it was when I got it from the impound yard. You'll need to get it out of here by the weekend. I have a big truck coming in for a total overhaul and I'll need the space. Sorry I couldn't be more help."

"You tried," said Marcia but she intended to locate another mechanic, one who had not heard of the case. The newspapers had trashed Debra for weeks and didn't seem to want to let up. Marcia hoped she could handle all that bad publicity.

The day that Debra was released was a happy day for the Wiebe's. Jerry was there to see her off but of course, the police were the ones to escort her back to jail. With Marcia's quick thinking though they knew that her time in could only be a matter of hours.

Debra got out of the police car at the courthouse just in time for the lunch whistle to sound. She stepped through the main doors, and waited for the search procedures but for some reason, maybe lunch, they decided to leave her alone. Hoping she would be put back in the same cell so she could see Suzette again, Debra walked briskly beside the guard. "Rumor has it, you didn't know that guy you iced," said the husky female beside her. "What happened anyway?"

"I don't know," said Debra.

146

"Well, I wish ya luck anyway."

"You do?"

"Sure, it wasn't premeditated. Something snapped. Hey, that could be me in there," she said as she unlocked the same cell Debra had been in before. "I get angry all the time."

Debra big round eyes conveyed all that she couldn't say with the guard's attitude as it was. She silently walked into the cell, put her basket of belongings on the bed and waited for the key to turn. Clang, clang, clang. She was back.

"Hi, Ya. Remember me?" came a voice from the next cell. "I hear yur getting out this afternoon. I hope it happens for ya. Did the shrink at Clarkville discover any answers yet?"

"Hi Suzette. Boy the rumor mill is going great guns in this place. How do you guys find out all this stuff?"

"We got nothing betta ta do. Do ya mean it's not true? Yur not gonna get out?"

"I don't know. My lawyer has arranged another hearing before the judge this afternoon but I don't know yet, nor does she, if it will get me out of here. We're hoping. What about you? Any word about your case?"

147

"Naw, I been through this before though. This is betta than livin at my place. No roaches."

"How is the Bible study coming that I left with you? Did you finish it and do you have any questions?'

"Naw, that woman that comes here every week helped me. Sherry used to be here too but she's changed so she wants to help the rest of us change. When I get out, we're going to live together and make a home for some others like us. We can keep each other straight."

"Boy that sounds great. I would sure like to keep in touch. If I do get out, can I come visit?"

"I don't know if they'll let you but you can sure try."

"Let's go for lunch. At least then we can see each other face to face." Debra said as the second whistle signifying their turn rang. Their doors all opened in unison and all the women located in Debra's area were allowed to visit the restroom and then go for lunch. March, march, march.

With lunch over, Debra lay down on her bunk to await the call for her turn in court. She prayed as she had never prayed before and Suzette prayed right along with her. Before long, a guard came to get her and he walked beside her to the courtroom, where Debra's family waited patiently. Since she had spent the last month in Clarkville, she was well rested and well groomed but that bright orange jumpsuit and handcuffs were not pleasant for anyone to see, let alone for Debra to wear.

The bailiff called everyone to order and the same judge who had ordered her to Clarkville stepped up to the large desk he used to look down upon the people he sent to prison. "Ms. Dixon, your client has been determined to be sane and competent to stand trial. Is that right?"

"Yes your honor. Here' s the evaluation filled out by Dr. Fry." Marcia handed the judge the sheaf of papers comprising the extensive evaluation that the Clarkville staff had performed for the court. "I wish to ask for this case to be dismissed since the prosecution have not been able to find any link between my client and the victim in this case. Since they cannot prove a capital case and that was what they charged her with, I wish to have the charges dropped."

"Your honor," whined the opposing lawyer.

The judge held up his hands. "Never mind," he said to the prosecutor. "Just sit down. Since your client has killed someone," he turned to Marcia, "and since your client has reached a favorable psychiatric evaluation, I will let a jury decide this case. In the meantime, since she has no prior record, and has not given anyone any problem since all this began, I will set the bail at $350,000. Mrs. Wiebe, that's a lot of money. If you do not appear before this bench," he looked at his calendar, "6 months from today, I will revoke your bail and you will lose the $35,000 bond that you will have to pay, do you understand me?"

"Yes your honor," she said amidst whooping and laughing from the courtroom.

"Settle down now," he looked sternly towards Debra's family, the cause of all the commotion. "I expect that you will all help your mother find out what happened and Mrs. Wiebe, I expect you to get help before your trial. If I have to order it I will but I think you are intelligent enough to know that your angry outbursts can't continue. That'll be all." And with that he slammed the gavel on his desk with a loud crash and walked out of the courtroom as everyone stood in respect for him.

All four children immediately surrounded Debra as well as her husband. They all hugged her and smiles were prevalent on everyone's face. It had been a long time since the Wiebe family had felt this good.

"Come on everyone, you too Marcia, let's go get some dinner. I know just the spot. Debra, go get out of that jumpsuit. I brought you your favorite pantsuit." Jerry could hardly believe they were letting her go after all this time.

"Marcia, we are just so grateful. You pulled it off."

"Not so fast, the work has just begun. We still don't have any answers as to why and without that the courts could send her away for a long time. Six months is not that far off." Marcia tried to calm their enthusiasm but to no avail. All six of them were oblivious to the scowls from the other side but Marcia hadn't missed a thing.

"You'd better get your client a magic genie if she thinks she going to beat this rap," snarled the prosecutor. "Nobody gets away with murder while I'm in office."

Marcia said nothing as she walked out behind the exuberant family. Even the black clothed older boys with their long hair and earrings were excited for their mother. Jail was a place for them, not their mother, they thought.

The dinner was a festive affair, with everyone talking at once and the children, especially the younger two, getting up every once in a while to hug their mother. Marcia watched and packed all this information away. In spite of the trials of raising kids, this was obviously one of the reasons why so many people did it.

When everyone left the restaurant to go their own way, she reminded Debra about the appointment with Mary at the counseling center. "We need to get started if we are to ever find out anything at all," she said, and then to herself, "If we do find out anything."

The Wiebe's headed for home leaving Marcia to follow a little while in her car before she turned to head for her house. The older boys accepted a ride as far as their end of town but took a bus from there. They wanted to do something else before going home.

Jerry and Debra held hands all the way much to the delight of the two in the back seat and soon they were pulling up into the driveway that Debra had left so angrily over a month before. The car door opened beside her and Debra slowly stepped out looking with such an intent gaze at their house that Jerry asked her what was wrong. "Nothing's wrong," she replied with emotion just below the surface of her voice. "I've just dreamt of this moment for so long that I want it to last. The house looks great, don't you think?"

Tears again. Boy would she ever quit crying? Debra walked up the front steps and into the house she could have lost forever and still might if Marcia was to be believed. For the next six months, she vowed, this family will know they are loved and they will get everything I've not given them for the past two years. Debra knew she had mistreated them and was determined never to yell or curse them again.

CHAPTER TWELVE

Almost three weeks later, Debra had not kept one appointment that Marcia had made with Mary and her outbursts were every bit as harsh as they had been before her jail time. She accused the kids of not loving her and Jerry of just saying he loved her to keep her quiet. Only the anger kept her from feeling that awful load of guilt.

Marcia was at her wits end. She knew there was something under all the temper but getting Debra to admit she needed help was like pulling teeth. Debra could actually forget for small amounts of time, the trauma she was facing. Jerry was careful what he said around her but she sensed he was feeling the tensions more than he let on. He seemed almost afraid of her next outburst.

Debra felt guilty over the atmosphere she was creating and even though her desire was for a peaceful home, she knew she was the cause of the present tensions. She didn't seem to be able to control the outbursts these days and so many things made her angry, most of them she felt were justified. Her Irish temper was controlling her instead of her controlling it but then she rationalized, anyone would be tense facing her present situation.

Her two younger children had been really well behaved since the incident but they didn't seem to be themselves either. She would catch them crying when they thought no one was watching and they seemed to always have a puzzled look on their faces. She supposed they were trying to understand how the mother they loved could have done such a thing but she was averse to discussing it with them. How could she help them to understand something she couldn't understand herself?

She loved them so much and the hurt she was inflicting on them made her want to just go away and let them live in peace. Maybe if she disconnected herself from them, they would be able to pretend she was dead. She wanted to be but she knew God would not look favorably on her suicide and running away from problems had never worked in the past. She believed that somehow God would see them through this trial but she dreaded to think of the way it would work out. There was no way this was not going to hurt the whole family more than it had already. The children were being teased at school and the newspapers were just now getting on with other news.

The jarring ring of the telephone intruded on her thoughts and she hastily answered it. "Hello!" She answered it in a less than receptive voice. "Hello," came the reply from her lawyer. "Is something the matter, Debra? This is Marcia."

Debra sighed heavily. "I wish people would quit asking me if everything was all right every time I open my mouth. I feel as if everyone is walking on eggshells around me, as if I might have a fit anytime. There's nothing wrong with me. I'm just so worried about the outcome of this trial."

"I don't want you to worry about that. I'll look after the worry, okay. You just pray and maybe get your hair done." Marcia was trying a feeble attempt at levity to raise her client's spirits but the joke was lost in the gravity of her situation. She felt that her chances, thus far, of acquittal were minimal and Debra spending time in prison was not going to be easy.

"I want you to see these people who may shed some light on why you behaved so out of character the other day.

Can I come over to tell you about them again, say about three this afternoon?"

"Sure. If they can explain my actions to me then I'll see them," Debra promised once again. "See you then. Bye for now." Debra was a little relieved. She spent the next hour doing all the housecleaning she had neglected the past two weeks. For now at least, her mind was at peace and she even began to hum as she dusted the furniture.

She started to pray, asking God to bring peace into her soul. She thanked Him for bringing Marcia to them when they needed her and for giving her such an understanding husband. She even thanked God for her oldest two children who had caused her to fall on her knees so often in the past four years.

She was at last able to see how God had taught her to rely more and more on Him, and although she was the independent type, she knew He was the center of her universe as never before. Even though she couldn't see Him, or touch Him, or feel Him, she knew He was real and that someday her kids would come back to Him as the Lord promised in the Bible.

The differences between her first two children and her second two were noticeable but each of her children were unique characters and she wouldn't trade their independent spirit for anything. She knew she and her husband had made a few mistakes raising each of them but they had honestly done their best with the information available to them. They had no guilt about their performance, only sorrow at the damage her children were doing to their own lives.

As parents, they had learned to relinquish the children to God, or at least were learning to on a daily basis. Especially in the past two weeks, with all of Debra's problems, they had to rely on God to deal with their kids.

As she worked, she remembered the first time she had discovered there really was a God and that the stories she had heard in Sunday school were not just stories. Her oldest, James was about fourteen months old and someone had loaned her a book to read. Reading was a passion but not one she had been free to indulge in since the birth of her active son. In his book, Hal Lindsay wrote about the end times and in the course of her reading it, she discovered her need of a Savior.

Debra remembered when she had decided to surrender that strong will of hers. She had used all sorts of excuses at first. She wasn't good enough or she was still having too much fun and didn't want to give up the social drinking or smoking, or she was too young. Then she learned that God hadn't asked her to give up anything and that she would never be good enough all by herself. It was only Christ living in her that would make her good enough and her priorities would change towards the things she then considered fun.

Since that time she had faithfully attended the only church she had known anything about which happened to be a nondenominational church. The preaching portrayed the Bible in all its truth and the attendees of that church tried hard to practice those teachings. As a black and white personality, she absorbed it all marveling at all the words and phrases that used to be so hard to understand and were now as clear as good quality, single pane glass.

God used many people to teach her things that other people grew up knowing and took for granted. Placing God back on the throne of her life was repeated time and again as she continued to take two steps forward but one step back due to her human nature and its fickleness. Where once she had thought she had surrendered all, she would learn that there was still a place she reserved for herself and so would have to surrender again. Growth in the Holy Spirit was a stage thing that required walking in the last step before proceeding on to the next.

Her husband and children joined her in her growing faith and they were, for a time, just as any other Christian family in the church. They had trials just like the others but nothing that took them away from their faith or really shook that faith. When the troubles started to come with adolescence, her oldest children were already into those teenage years and she thought they had escaped those pressures. She learned what smug' and 'complacency' was as their faith underwent the ravages of an earthquake that would record an 8 or 9 on the Richter scale. Satan attacked where they, especially she, was most vulnerable, her children. He found her Achilles' heel and used it to the fullest.

It was then she discovered this anger, a rage so deep that her very soul was incapable of keeping it under control. Some said she reacted all out of proportion to the incidences in her life but, she was convinced, that anyone experiencing the same circumstances would react the same. She raged at her husband and he would appear frightened at times when his wife seemed so out of control. Her younger children became silent, uncommunicative and her older children only wanted to be out of there. Most of the time she would be herself, of course; but when someone did something to upset her, she was inconsolable and fierce. Then everyone knew she had proud Scottish and Irish ancestry and weren't THEY always loud when THEY got angry.

The doorbell interrupted her reflections. What was that expression, 'Saved by the bell'? It never felt too good to be reflective. As she opened the door to Marcia, she felt optimistic and wished Jerry could be there.

"Come and sit down. Would you like a cup of coffee or would some iced tea sound better? I just made both." Debra looked forward to the visit as she had not looked forward to many things in the last weeks.

She looks to be in better spirits than when I talked with her on the phone thought Marcia, but I am still concerned about what I have to tell her. Marcia knew Debra still didn't really believe she could be sent to prison. Her client was expecting some glitch in the law or some...oh, maybe,…Savior, to perform the miracle of making all this go away.

"I'll take the iced tea, if you don't mind, Debra. I'm all coffee-ed out already today." Marcia wanted to get this conversation over with and clear up any misconceptions Debra might have.

"I was just thinking back to the time when I accepted the Lord into my life years ago," Debra began. "Have you ever thought about your need of a Savior, Marcia? You may think you're self sufficient, but everyone has a need to be with God. We were created with that need and so often try to fill it with other things, such as work or material possessions." Debra had always had a strong desire to tell others about her faith and she knew that she wouldn't get a better chance with Marcia.

"We need to concentrate on your defense now, Debra, but someday we will talk about this faith of yours. Come and sit while I explain what I have discovered. You know that our biggest problem is going to be defending an act that seemingly has no motive. The jury won't go for the accident angle since there was an eyewitness and a police officer at the scene. We have to find that other defense."

"I know, I know, you've told me all this before," snapped Debra reverting to her quick temper once again.

"I made another appointment with the Christian Counseling Center on Seneca and the woman there thinks that the rage you feel is the angle we need to explore. The other person is Dr. Fry and you know that you get along well with him. He wants you to come for some extensive therapy to explore reasons for this anger as well. Both these people want what's best for you. How about I pick you up tomorrow morning and we go visit them?" Marcia's fingers were crossed for she knew this was not what Debra wanted to hear.

"There has been no sign of mental illness in my family at all so you can just forget that angle. Do you think that the only defense is insanity? I'm incensed that you would even explore that possibility. I'm a God fearing, Christian woman and Satan doesn't control me in any way. That's what insanity is, you know, Satan. Forget it! Just forget it!!" As her rage grew, she picked up a vase and as Debra raised it to launch it at the astonished lawyer; Jerry walked in the front door.

"What's going on here? Debra, honey, calm down. Marcia, what's happened? Has Debra's case gotten worse? Somebody say something, please!" Jerry was shouting now and he dreaded the time he would come home to a window smashed or worse. What was happening to his wife? Where was this anger coming from?

Debra was screaming now as she explained Marcia's proposed course of action. Jerry held her tight and pretty soon her body grew more relaxed and she started to cry in frustration. Debra didn't cry very often but when she was this angry, her inability to act on her anger would bring tears. "Let's look at this calmly for a minute." Jerry was ever the peacemaker and peace was all he wanted from life. Sometimes Debra felt he sacrificed too much for that peace but this time she was willing to let him set the tone. "Debra, the judge said that you need to get help. You' re destroying this family. Please honey…" Jerry sat down, placed his head in his hands and let the tears of frustration come. Seeing her husband so defeated, Debra began to listen.

Marcia began by going over the details of their case. She treated them as one for she knew that whatever punishment Debra would receive, Jerry would experience the same.

They were a close couple and would suffer terribly from the separation they faced as well as the trauma of the trial and publicity.

"So you see, this is not going to just disappear," Marcia continued. "Whether you want to admit it or not, the fact is that you did kill someone and society demands payment for that crime. We need to explore the reasons. We all know that until recently, you were incapable of the kind of rage it takes to do what you did. Mary, at the counseling center, feels that maybe you were abused as a child and the rage you feel is a result of that. She says they are now discovering that even a small child as young as 3 months old, when abused, feels anger but because they are unable to do anything with that anger, they stuff it or suppress it. Then later in life, usually as a teenager, it erupts."

Marcia went on to further describe the plans she had been working on to exonerate her client. "From Jonathan's perspective, a trauma could explain the loss of memory and abuse in childhood is traumatic, isn't it, to the child experiencing it. Once we have their evaluations, we will know how to proceed." Marcia hoped this fact would force

Debra to come to terms with her situation since they needed her to see the seriousness of what she was facing.

"What would my defense be? What happens if they find me guilty by reason of insanity? Will I be incarcerated in a nut house and for how long? I'm really scared." Her trembling was visible and as Jerry and Marcia tried to reassure her, Debra fought the tears threatening to leak out of her eyelids. Crying had never helped anything, or so she thought, and she always fought hard to contain them. It always made her angrier to cry since she saw tears as a sign of weakness.

"For one thing, it will be temporary insanity since we have already had you evaluated for the insanity plea and you are not insane. A temporary condition is all we will find, I am sure. We'll know more after we talk to the experts. Will I pick you up tomorrow?" Marcia wanted to move, now that her client was so calm but she was beginning to understand a little of what Jerry had to put up with. Something was definitely not right here and she hoped that Mary or Jonathan could get to the bottom of what was causing these outbursts. Marcia was sure that was the explanation needed to defend Debra but whether the jury would understand that explanation, was another matter.

"Set up the appointments Marcia. If tomorrow works, let's do it," Jerry intervened. "I'll take the time off work to go with you, Deb, and we'll get to the bottom of this. We know you're going to spend time away from home for a while, but the less the better, eh? After all, if there is something that causes you to fly off the handle so easily, we need to pinpoint it and eradicate it. The kids and I are affected by it, as well as you. Lately your ministry for the Lord has suffered too. You've been so wrapped up in all the mess here that you haven't done much in that area at all. Honey, I'm sorry you're the one going through this but the sooner we look at the possibilities, the sooner we can look forward to a regular life again." Jerry hugged her as he gave Marcia the thumbs up sign. "Go for it, Marcia. I know my wife is not a cold blooded killer and the sooner we can prove that to the people of this state, the better."

CHAPTER THIRTEEN

As they saw Marcia to her car, Jerry and Debra walked arm in arm. This was all so distressing and yet they knew that God was there with them every step of the way. Debra was having trouble reconciling her temper flare-ups with her faith and she was sure many others in the church would not be able to equate one with the other either.

As they re-entered their small but tastefully decorated home, Debra asked, "Do you think all that strict punishment from my father could have been abuse? I know that no one else I knew experienced any of the same things but I'm sure there was no sexual abuse or stuff like that. When that child development specialist I saw years ago told me that I had the potential to abuse and that my father had abused me, I thought that by giving all that over to the Lord that it would be finished. I never really believed that the doctor was right anyway. After all I haven't followed the pattern of abused children. Most women from abuse backgrounds marry a man who continues the abuse. I didn't but then I've always believed that the Lord arranged our marriage. Whenever I would get angry with the kids I worked really hard at controlling my temper and even though I failed once in awhile, the kids were not abused. In fact when Marcia was asking me all those questions about my growing up years, I never even thought about that time in our marriage. Now it appears all I did was stuff it…only for it to come back now. It's like dirty baggage that I've brought into this marriage that won't go away." Debra felt like a piece of soiled, damaged goods, and a detriment to her family.

Jerry hugged her. "There's no use speculating until we see the specialists. Besides you can't help what your father did to you. There's not much can be done about it after all these years either. I'm sure there are other people, even in our church, who come from harsher backgrounds than you do and they have learned to put it behind them and get on with their lives. We'll do the same. Let's get supper started. The kids will be getting hungry. Hey, I know…why don't we go out to eat tonight? A break from all this is just what we need." Jerry shouted for the kids to get cleaned up so they could leave, and Debra went to their room to change into something a little tidier.

Jerry had some time to reflect on his wife and, not for the first time, he thought how lucky he was. She tried so hard most of the time to be the kind of wife God wanted her to be. She was smart, organized, a hard worker, innovative, and she believed in Him no matter what. When their business had failed a few years ago, she was the one who had kept things going when he fell apart. She remained strong and supportive when he needed it and now it was his turn to support her.

She was loyal and he never heard her say anything to make him feel stupid or less of a man in front of other people. In fact she was always building him up and making him feel like a real man. She had been a good wife and he thanked God every day for her. He was looking forward to their evening out, since she enjoyed not having to cook once in a while.

The kids came clambering down the stairs ready for an evening out. As Jerry saw his wife and life partner approach, she never failed to make him feel proud of her. She always tried to look her best for him and this night was no exception. Jerry locked the door as his family walked toward the car parked in the driveway. Getting in beside Debra, he turned on the ignition, backed down the driveway and out onto the street. They were on their way to the Red Lobster, not his favorite place to eat but everyone else's.

After Marcia left the Wiebe's home, she went straight to her office. Waiting for her, in her outer office, was Jonathan and he grinned as she walked in. Her eyebrows lifted in a questioning smile but she was glad to see him. "What brings you to the big city and so soon yet?" she asked. "Missing something for that country clinic of yours?

"I needed to consult with one of your fancy city doctors, that's all and I thought we could fit in that drink you mentioned the other day when you called. Besides, I wanted to see you again. We had so much fun the last time we were together. Do you have time today?" Jonathan was dressed in a pair of beige slacks and a sports shirt open at the neck. His eyes shone as he watched Marcia, wondering if she was as glad to see him as she appeared.

He'd never succeeded in acting coy when he was younger and now that he had grown as a physician and as a person, he saw no reason to play games now either. He had thought of waiting a while to come to the city to see her again since he didn't want to rush things but then figured

171

"what the heck". He wanted to see her and he thought she felt the same way so why not?

"I'd like that too but first let's clear up some business. Remember Debra Wiebe? Well, I just left her house and she has agreed to an appointment. Oh, and Jonathan, I hope you can fit her in soon. She's really volatile and the tensions are straining their marriage."

"Marcia, how does tomorrow sound? I was thinking of staying in the city tonight anyway so I could see her first thing in the morning. In the meantime we could have dinner this evening, or do you have some other plans?" Jonathan hadn't had a day off in a long time. He had become a workaholic since the breakup of his marriage and now, he felt, was an opportunity to break that trend.

"I'll have to phone my client but if you'd like to sit here for a few minutes, I won't be long." She walked into her private office as he sat in the most comfortable chair in her waiting room. As soon as she was seated at her desk she dialed the Wiebe's. Their answering machine answered on the fourth ring.

"Hello, Jerry, this is Marcia. How does tomorrow at 9 a.m. sound for Debra to see Jonathan Fry? He's here in my office and tells me he plans to spend the night in the city. It would save you a trip to the country if Debra could see him then. I'm sure she would like to get this over with. Phone me if these plans don't work, otherwise we'll be expecting you both at 9 a.m. here at my office."

"I have an outside appointment at that time so Jonathan will have privacy for his visit with Debra. Just come straight in and he'll be here to meet you both. Bye for now." Marcia decided to make the other appointment as well so she dialed the counseling center and straightened her desk as she waited for them to answer. She hoped they could fit the Wiebe's in tomorrow as well.

"Hello, may I speak with Mary, please? Yes I'll hold." Mary was just finishing with a client so she put her phone down and went to explain to Jonathan that the arrangements had been made. He told her to take whatever time she needed so she returned to her desk and picked up her phone just as Mary answered on the other end.

"Sorry to keep you waiting, Ms. Dixon," Mary said. "What can I do for you?"

"My client has agreed to see you finally and this time her husband is bringing her so she can't get cold feet. If you could fit them in tomorrow, it would sure expedite matters."

"Debra needs to want to get better so I hope she is coming with that in mind and not because she's being forced. I'm looking in my appointment book now and I see I have an opening for 10 in the morning and another at 1 P.M." Mary was sure she could help solve this mystery for these people. More and more of the populace were seeking help from child abuse and setting right what had once been so wrong in their lives. She was seeing whole families benefit from one patient's therapy.

"One in the afternoon would be better. They have an appointment with Jonathan Fry of the Clarkville Psychiatric Facility for the morning. With both of your opinions, we'll stand a better chance of understanding this rage of hers. Debra just about beaned me today in a temper flare-up. The sooner she gets help the better."

"I'll see them then at 1 P.M. tomorrow and I hope we can get to the bottom of this, too. The type of behavior you describe plays havoc with the family." Mary hung up and Marcia returned to the waiting room to see Jonathan.

"Are you sure you want to go for dinner tonight?" she asked. "I wouldn't want you to be too tired for that appointment tomorrow morning." She teased him knowing he was not going to be too tired. In fact he looked to her to be full of energy and seemed to be excited about the prospect of their seeing each other again. As they walked out the door of her office, he reached for her hand and giving it a squeeze, he conveyed just how un-tired he really was.

"Shall we take my car or yours," he asked when they emerged on the street in front of Marcia's office building. "Why not take yours," she answered. "It's been a while since I was driven anywhere by a man and the last time we met, I drove. I know this little place just across from the zoo that would be quiet, a nice place for us to talk without any interruptions."

"That sounds nice. I feel as if we've been seeing each other for a long time, as if we never lost touch at all." Jonathan opened the passenger door of his beat-up old 58 Chevy, a classic and one that he hoped he could refurbish some day.

"I see that you still have this old car!" said Marcia. "This is going to bring back some wonderful memories." She laughed as she recalled an incident when they had been with friends in this car years ago and they spent the entire ride to the restaurant reliving the past. The drive was far too short but soon they were seated at a corner table overlooking the zoo across the street. It was quiet at this time of day but they could see animals of all shapes and sizes eating food provided by attendants earlier in the evening.

"This has always been a favorite place for me," said Marcia. "I love watching the animals and imagining them in their natural environment. It's too bad they are caged here but for some of them, this means they get to live instead of being hunted for their coats or their ivory."

"I guess I never knew that you were so fond of animals," he interjected. "Before my divorce, I dreamed of one day owning an acreage and having a couple of horses. I have always loved the smell and the feel of power when I ride a horse. Now, of course, that dream is just that, a dream. I find it easier to just live on campus at the hospital."

"You're young yet. Don't you think you'll ever re-marry?" Marcia couldn't imagine feeling fatalistic about that aspect of her life. Even though she had never found that special someone, she knew that it was a matter of time for her.

"Right now, I still feel too damaged but I suppose if the right person came along. I have dated a couple of times but I always felt uncomfortable around them, as if I didn't have enough to offer them."

"Oh, pooh! You have a lot to offer." As she said it she knew it was true and that he had a lot to offer her as well. The thought took her breath away for a second but she hoped her face didn't give her away.

The waiter arrived with the menu and for the next ten minutes, both silently stared at it but with thoughts entirely unrelated to eating going through their heads. Jonathan was thinking back to the time when he had thought this woman was his soul-mate. Her hectic schedule coupled with his when they were both trying so hard to earn their degrees, had come between them. They just never seemed to have time for each other.

When they had gone out though, it had always been fun. He enjoyed this woman's company then and he still did now. She was smart, very nice to look at, and she had a great sense of humor. Glancing back at the menu, he sighed. This was going to be a fun ride.

On the other side of the table Marcia's thoughts mirrored Jonathan's. She had a little trouble with the fact that he was a divorced man since that meant a lot of baggage but he was great to look at, had a quirky sense of humor, and really seemed to care about people. His intelligence did not get in the way of their having fun together either. We'll just have to wait and see, she thought, as she too looked towards the choices available from the menu.

Once they had ordered, he a chicken dish and she a seafood pasta entrée, the waiter brought them a loaf of 'warm from the oven' sourdough bread and a house salad. Both Jonathan and Marcia added dressing and began to eat. In between bites though they kept up a steady stream of conversation.

"How come you never had kids?" asked Marcia.

"Stacie never wanted any. She made it clear right from the beginning that her career was her baby and when we first met and married I thought that was okay for me too. But after a couple of years, I would look around and see families playing together or even just riding in a car and I knew I would never be happy without children of my own. That was probably the beginning of the end for us, although neither Stacie nor I realized it at the time. She remained true to herself as she was always so quick to remind me but I had changed."

"Sometimes we say and think things when we are young that we realize as we get older was premature. I used to think that my career was all I needed but now I'm not so sure."

"Have you ever thought of children of your own?"

"Lately, I have a number of times. I'm not getting any younger but I love what I do. Would it be fair to children to have them but ask a day care provider to raise them? I'm not sure what the answer is."

"It is a dilemma for a lot of couples, I am sure but somehow they still seem to manage. I don't know the answer either."

"It's a moot point for me anyway since I've never found Mr. Right. If it's in the cards or as Debra would say, "If God wills it," then it'll happen but for now…I am just happy to be here with you having a conversation about something other than work. How about you?"

"Work can be all consuming sometimes. Most of my free time is spent with some of the other doctors and their wives so we are always talking shop. It bores the women to tears so they gather elsewhere and have their own discussions. I like to be able to leave that all behind me once in a while too."

"When you were in college, you participated in some sports. Do you still run or snow ski or any of the other things you did? You were always into something."

"I run every day actually. It helps me think clearer and keeps me from getting that middle aged spread thing that a lot of guys have happen to their once agile bodies. I also go for a weekend or two every year to Aspen, where the best ski-ing in the world happens. Do you snow-ski?'

"I took lessons a couple of years ago and spend a little time on the slopes every year. I've never been to Aspen though. That sounds like a great way to spend a weekend."

"Maybe you and I will have to go together sometime," Jonathan said with a gleam in his eye. They were finding more and more things that they liked in common as their conversation progressed.

The rest of the evening went along the same way. When the food arrived both ate with relish enjoying every morsel. Marcia had always had a good appetite and yet she never seemed to gain any weight while Jonathan might like food but his regular exercise regimen was needed to keep him fit.

Over coffee their conversation continued into the late evening hours leaving little time for long goodnights when Jonathan dropped Marcia back where her car was parked. She watched from the inside as he drove off, wishing she could spend more time with him tomorrow but knowing that after she let him into her office, she had too much work to do to keep her there. Sometimes being a lawyer got in the way, she whined inwardly.

CHAPTER FOURTEEN

The next morning dawned clear and sunny with a forecast for rain showers in the early afternoon. The Wiebe household rose about seven a.m. to get ready on time for Debra's appointments. The children were old enough now to stay on their own for a couple of hours but Jerry was a worry wart, so they had arranged for them to spend time with their grandmother, Jerry's mom, who just happened to live across the street from their school. Since neither Debra nor Jerry knew how long they would be away that day, Jerry had taken the entire day off work and they could rely on his mom to keep the kids until they could pick them up, whenever that would be.

Breakfast was a hurried affair and some of the joking around that had disappeared in the last few days resurfaced. Matthew, their youngest son, liked to tease his younger sister and she was at an age where she was sensitive to some of it. He liked to tickle her but she hurt so easily and his hands were so big already. He was going to be a big man when he grew up.

"Are they going to put you into one of those sanitations, Mom?" Cindy asked. "What are we going to do without you here? How long will you be gone?" She was full of questions and her parents could sense her fears.

"Sanitarium, Cindy and no, not yet anyway. Today is just a meeting with the specialists to try and determine why your mother can't remember what happened. Whatever happens, we will keep you kids informed and don't forget the Lord is still with us. Why don't we pray about this right now and ask the Lord to guide these people in their assessment of your Mom? Also we want the Lord to bring us peace about this situation." Her father wanted only to wipe away all of their fears but they were too in tune to the household comings and goings to be fooled anymore.

When they were really little, it was so easy to keep unpleasant things from them but now, they had to reassure their children the only way they knew how and prayer always helped as they focused on their Lord instead of their problems.

As they bowed their heads, a peace descended even to Debra and their love of God, for a time, took over. They loved each other through their prayers and always found that when their focus was on the Lord, they could think more clearly as things fell into perspective. The Bible was so clear about Jesus as their focal point during trials and tribulations and it had taken the trials of the years past to help them fully understand this concept. The 'rest' they found in their Lord could not be attained by any other means and as long as they kept their priorities straight, they knew God would continue to help them endure this latest test of their faith.

"We'd better hurry now or we'll be late," interjected Debra. "You kids help your grandmother around the house a little. Matthew, if you see that the lawn needs mowing, maybe she'll let you do that. Cindy, even at your age you know how to run a vacuum or dust furniture. Vacuuming can be a chore for your grandma, so why not ask her if you could do that for her?" Debra was always trying to organize everyone and Jerry smiled at his wife's return to her old self, if only for a little while. He gently pinched her cheek and his smile reminded her that she was still special to him.

The scurry of everyone rushing to get dressed filled the next half-hour and before they knew it they were sitting in the car on their way to the older Mrs. Wiebe's house to drop off the children. The radio was playing some soft music and they all seemed to be content to listen and let their thoughts wander as they gazed out the windows of the car.

Cindy began thinking about the time two years ago when her older brother had run away from home. It had taken her parents several days to find him. The pain in her parent's eyes then, had seemed invisible but now their pain was something you could reach out and touch. At only six, it was hard to watch because she knew there was nothing she could do.

Her love for her parents made her want to hit out at the people perpetrating this pain and yet, from the little she knew, it seemed they could not deny her mother's part in this current problem. Her older brothers seemed not to care how much they hurt their parents but she knew they did care in their own way. They had called almost every day since the accident and planned to stand by their Mom at the trial, if there was one. Cindy hoped that today they would find a way to avoid the trial and just get their mother into treatment.

Cindy couldn't help but reflect on all the anger she had seen in her home in the short years since she was old enough to know what anger was all about. First, her older brothers were the ones always mad at each other and they often directed their anger toward Matthew or her. She could even remember the time when those big boys fought over her and pulled her arms out of joint by playing tug of war using her body as the rope. Boy, were her parents ever angry that time.

Their wrestling had broken some furniture one time when they were supposed to be babysitting her and Matthew, she recalled, and Dad had made them get part-time jobs to pay for it. Each blamed the other though and they never did learn from that incident. When they left home, Mom and Dad were sad but Cindy reflected, things were kind of pleasant around the house for the first time she could ever remember. But then Mom's temper tantrums began. It was as if she had given herself permission to be angry about everything.

The familiar street that her grandmother lived on was in sight and her reflections took on a newer bent. Her grandmother was not too supportive, she knew, of her Mom and she hoped she wouldn't say anything to make her mother angry. She started to wave as she saw her grandmother on her front steps and as soon as the car stopped they were out, waving their parents off. Thank goodness a confrontation had been avoided. Both children loved being at their grandmother's place. They smiled at her and then went into her cozy home to wait until they had to leave for school.

Jerry and Debra were quick to leave his mother's house since they wanted to stop for a quick cup of coffee before arriving at their first appointment. They could now voice their concerns about pursuing this course of action since the kids had been dropped off, but neither seemed inclined to begin. Lost in their own thoughts all they could do was silently support one another. The streets were crowded at this time of day. Everyone wanted to get to work at the same time. Horns blared and brakes grinded, as drivers cut each other off. Rush hour, whether morning or evening, was not pleasant to drive through.

Over coffee Jerry began their conversation. "Honey, I love you. No matter what happens I will be by your side. Please, don't ever forget that." Jerry wanted to, one last time, reassure her and Debra looked at him and smiled.

"I was just thinking about the older children, Jerry, and wondering when they were going to get smart. Whenever we talk to those older two it's like talking to someone from another planet. We raised them to behave within certain guidelines but it doesn't seem to matter anymore what they were taught. They live as if they never heard of decency, hard work, or morals." Debra was reminded of the phone call she received last night when one of her sons dropped another bombshell.

"Honey, we have enough on our plates without worrying over what these kids of ours are doing. Let's just concentrate on the task at hand and let our children work out their own problems or at least allow the Lord to teach them through it." Jerry had the ability, it seemed, to be able to separate himself from his kids for a time but Debra couldn't. The sorrow of their lives filled her days and nights and she continued to want to solve all of their problems for them, like when they were 10 years old. She knew God wanted her to relinquish them but they kept their parents involved by their constant distress calls.

"How can I not respond when our son tells us he is throwing up any food he does eat because of his non-existent diet?" Her voice rose in irritation. She did what she believed any other parent would do and put together a hamper of food for them to eat regularly at least once a week, only to find out that her son has been spending most of his time living at his girlfriend's house, in her bed.

"It just gets worse every day." Her frustration and anger began to boil. "Maybe it would all be for the best if I was locked up and you all just divorced me. The whole family, I mean. I don't seem to be able to cope with all these catastrophes and my first reaction is always to get angry. I know that anger never helps anything but it surfaces so quickly that I'm shouting at someone before I know what's happening."

The knot was back and Debra was trying to run again, as she had wanted to do since the problems began. Prison would enable her to shut out the sorrows in her children's lives if she were no longer available to them. Carrying around this heavy heart made life anything but pleasant and there seemed to be no end to it. The only time she had ever been able to divorce herself from the events marking the last few years was when they were on holidays and those happened all too infrequently in their lives.

Jerry watched as his wife wrung her hands repeatedly in agitation. Obviously this coffee break did not help matters but then maybe if Jonathan could see her in this state, he would be able to give a more accurate diagnosis. They left the coffee shop then and returned to the task of getting to their appointment on time.

Debra's thoughts were brought to an end when they pulled into the parking lot for the building housing the law firm Marcia Dixon worked for. They were both nervous although they wanted to get this over with. The climb up the long flight of stairs at the entrance to this massive building kept their thoughts occupied. They boarded the elevator and when they stepped out, Dr. Jonathan Fry was there to meet them. "Hello, Debra. It's good to see you again. Jerry we've never met formally but I saw you once or twice when you came to visit Debra at the hospital. Let's go into Marcia's office and get re-acquainted, shall we?"

As they sat on chairs drawn together in a circle, Debra was the first to speak. "Dr. Fry, have you ever known anyone else to commit the kind of crime I am accused of but then not remember the commission of that crime?"

Debra wanted to get right to the point and Jonathan could sense her agitation.

"Debra, do you have some misgivings about being here?" he asked.

"Not any more than anyone else would have being dragged before a psychiatrist. I'm not insane, remember," she griped.

"No you're not but then not everyone I see is. I help people resolve their feelings, help them put things into perspective, you might say. Now, first I want to find out a little about you both from a more personal viewpoint than we were able to discuss before. Then if Jerry doesn't mind, I'd like to talk to you alone. We'll get to your question in due course. Now fill me in on the last few years and then we can go on from there," Jonathan engineered the discussion.

For the next hour both Jerry and Debra talked about the traumas in their life and what their hopes and dreams had been for their family. Jerry seemed able to talk clinically but Debra's feelings were always just under the surface, sometimes forcing Jerry to talk more than Jonathan would have liked. She displayed tears some of the time but for the most part, her answers were harsh, filled with anger.

The Wiebes left nothing out and as they talked, Dr. Fry could sympathize with them. They'd had a hard time of it and although Jonathan had no kids of his own, he could almost understand the anguish they suffered. There was more to the pain than just what their sons had done though. An underlying tension, not relevant to this problem, was exacerbating the issues at hand. Jonathan couldn't quite put his finger on it, at this point anyway. Debra would need a lot more sessions.

"Jerry, would you mind leaving us for the time being? Debra and I need to zero in on the memory loss and the fewer distractions we have the better." As Jerry closed the door behind him, Jonathan asked Debra if she could remember anything over the past two years that would be traumatic in nature, more than she had divulged so far.

"I'm not sure what you mean by traumatic, Dr. Fry. I find that the behavior of my kids is traumatic but to pinpoint one incident more than the others, I just don't know."

"What about that morning? Can you remember what happened from the time you got out of bed that morning until the police arrested you? What were you thinking during the drive?" Debra started to tell him the details of her day and as she inadvertently left out a detail or two, he would prompt her with questions. Finally they reached the point of the accident itself.

"I was driving along thinking about the boys as usual, swerving to avoid hitting other cars and I saw this long-haired boy standing at the bus stop." Debra expounded.

"Why were you avoiding other cars? Were there some accidents alone the route?" Jonathan was curious about her description of that day.

"No accidents yet, but the way some of those men drive! If I hadn't avoided them they would have hit me and of course, being men, they would have then blamed me. THEY talk about women drivers." Her 'harrumph' was very audible and Jonathan, being the professional that he was, didn't miss a thing.

"Your opinion of men is pretty low. Have you always thought this badly of men? How has your attitude played itself out in front of your family?"

"I've never really thought about it that much. I've always felt intimidated when dealing with men as if I wasn't qualified enough in whatever I was doing. Maybe it's because I don't trust them. They're always doing something that appears so stupid that I feel that at times I just don't understand them. I trust my husband. We're just fine. It's not been an issue in our home." Debra was quick, a little too quick, to reassure him on that point.

"Okay, let's go on. When had you first met this 'long-haired' kid? Why did you dislike him so much?" Jonathan wanted to get to the heart of the matter.

"I have never seem him before in my life. I felt he was probably disappointing his family just as my kids were but I had no reason to dislike him personally. The last thing I remember is seeing him standing at the bus stop. Next I was being hand cuffed to my steering wheel by a big burly cop. I'm not even sure I hit that kid, but the police officer would have no reason for lying, would he?"

"I just can't understand what happened. I'm scared. Doctor, can you help me?" Confiding in this man felt so strange to Debra but she knew that from what Marcia had said that she needed him on her side. She felt the fear bring a lump to her throat but there was no way she was going to cry here.

"The trauma in your life must be a little way back. Let's explore further, shall we?" For the next hour, Debra answered questions and would sometimes volunteer information as she became more comfortable with Dr. Fry again. She discovered that, although he was not seeking to evaluate her for the state that he had a quick mind and had the ability to zero in on areas of her life that she had not thought about for a long time. When she told him of a child development expert assessment that she had been abused as a child, he concurred.

"You show all the signs of one suffering from delayed traumatic syndrome, such as one might experience from abuse but you don't seem to agree with that assessment, do you? Let's set up a series of appointments. Clarkville is not too far away. We could meet once a week and then see what we discover. I know that Marcia wants you to plead not guilty, using the temporary insanity defense and since you never knew that person and can't remember the incident, it appears likely but we won't have a clear picture until we've met a few more times. What do you think?"

Debra's body language indicated that she was feeling trapped. Her eyes darted from side to side looking for an answer and wishing she didn't have to give one. She could not get over that a psychiatrist felt she needed to see him for more sessions. Of course, she had to admit, she also was having a hard time fathoming the fact that she had killed someone. Maybe this would be a way she could take back control of her life. By allowing the doctor to investigate her past or future or whatever he will dig into, she could move ahead instead of feeling like she was stuck in a volcano just before it erupted.

"Once you are processed through the court system," he continued, "they will probably recommend that you spend some time in our facility anyway. This way we will be one step ahead of them and you will be able to demonstrate to the court your willingness to deal with your emotions in a more productive way. For now though, this is all we can accomplish today. You are not crazy, but there is something that needs looking after." Jonathan knew how she felt about the possibility of someone reading her wrong but he was confident that he would be able to build the rapport necessary to help her.

"Okay doctor, let me know how soon you want me to begin. I'll wait for a call from your secretary and we'll set up some appointments. Do you have any idea how many times I'll need to come?"

"Not yet. Why don't we plan to play it by ear and each week you'll make another appointment until there is no need to. Let's try for the beginning of next week…say Wednesday about 1 p.m." he said as he looked through his appointment calendar, a tool he never left home without.

"That sounds okay to me. The courts have suspended my license though so I'll need to arrange a ride every time but I am sure that Jerry can work longer hours some days to cover the extra time he will need to take off. I've become such a burden to him," she sighed hanging her head.

"He loves you. Anyone can see that. I'm sure he wants nothing better than for you to resolve some of those pent up feelings and is more than happy to help you do that. See you next Wednesday, okay?" Jonathan added as he ushered her out the door and into the care and protection of her husband.

As Jerry and Debra left Marcia's office, some of the spring that had disappeared from Debra's walk over the past two years was back. "You know, just talking to someone makes me feel less like a cement truck with a load of cement. Why don't we find a cozy place to get some lunch?"

It had been a long morning and they still had to see Mary at one that afternoon. They drove around for a while trying to decide where the best place for them to eat was when they noticed a sign advertising a special new restaurant that they had never been in before.

"Let's go there," said Debra. They had always enjoyed trying new places to eat when they had had the time to date, before the children had required so much of their time.

"That's a great idea. We haven't taken the time to just be together for a long time and now we could sure use the distraction," added Jerry.

It took them a while to find the location but the ride around the city was worth the effort. They watched people walking on the sidewalks and enjoyed seeing some new businesses along the way. Since they had to be at the Christian Counseling Center by one o'clock, they knew they had no time to dawdle but resolved to take a day for themselves soon when they could sightsee and shop.

"There it is," announced Debra, pointing to a small building that still looked like it smelled of fresh paint. They parked along the street nearby and walked across to enter a brightly lit room where a few others were waiting or so it seemed.

"How long will we have to wait?" Jerry asked the hostess by the door.

"Oh, none sir...would you like smoking or non-smoking?

"Non—smoking, please," he replied. She showed them to their booth immediately and soon they were perusing a lengthy menu of delicious choices.

CHAPTER FIFTEEN

Seated in a secluded part of the restaurant, Jerry and Debra planned to enjoy this lunch to the fullest. It had been so long since they had taken the time to be together, just the two of them. Whenever one had the opportunity, the other seemed to be busy so that getting together had been impossible. It was rather sad that these circumstances should afford them the appropriate interlude.

They placed their order and a companionable silence was followed by a slow start at conversation. During the days when they had dated while the children were younger, the rule had been that they could not talk about the kids when they went out. By unspoken agreement, that same rule applied now especially since Jerry was afraid it would trigger a negative response in his wife. However, the topic of the kids soon reared its head but was directed at the younger two.

"The kids have been very quiet lately and they seem to spend a lot of time in their rooms," began Debra. "I have noticed that the minute we differ on anything, they go upstairs."

"They've been doing that for a while now," added Jerry. "I think they are afraid we will come to hate each other and get a divorce just like most of the parents of their school-mates."

"This situation is so complex," she said. "I really don't understand why I get so angry over simple things. And I have not been sleeping well lately, or for at least the last couple of months."

"Why didn't you say something about that to me. I could have helped, I think, with that problem." Jerry was not used to his wife keeping things from him and he didn't like to think of her experiencing anything that would hurt her health.

"A lot of people,...women I know...seem to have problems sleeping sometimes. It's not so unusual, is it? But I suppose it does make me more irritable."

"Irritable!!! Honey, you have been so on edge, we are all walking on egg shells, these days." Just then, lunch was placed before them. "Let's forget all about that though for now. We will deal with the situation enough over the next weeks until the trial. Let's just think about you and I. I've missed you, don't you know and I want us to get some of that closeness back."

Their conversation took a different route after that on to less stressful subjects and the time flew by. Talk such as his work, her need for some new clothes, their need to visit with the children's teachers and others enabled them to forget, just for a minute, what they were facing. By the time they left, they had strengthened their resolve to not allow any of this mess to come between them.

Leaving a generous tip for the waitress, and walking out into the sunshine, they smiled at each other. Jerry opened the car door for her and Debra felt just like a newly wed for the first time in a very long, long time. As they got into the car Debra said, "I love you, Jerry. I really appreciate your support."

"I love you too, Debra and the support is all part of the promises I made to you on our wedding day. We promised 'for better or worse' and I meant that then and still do." Jerry believed in marriage in general but his in particular and to him it was inconceivable that anyone would not behave in this manner.

The short ride to the Christian Counseling Center seemed longer since the traffic appeared to be heavier at this time of day. When they entered the building, Victoria, the receptionist very quickly made them feel right at home, offering them a comfortable chair and some coffee. When they were ushered into Mary's office, it also had a comfortable feel to it that immediately put people at ease. The soft hues of gray and pink blended to enhance the rapport necessary for this kind of counseling.

She offered them more coffee and the Wiebes were pleased to have something to do with their hands. Their nerves were on edge but Mary was used to a client's first time jitters so she increased her attempts to put them at ease. She dealt with them differently than Dr. Fry had in that she simply asked them how their day had been and what they were thinking about.

As they talked, she asked a lot about how they felt in given circumstances. She discovered enough to decide that counseling would be extensive since there did indeed seem to be problems left over from Debra's childhood. These problems had been reflected in how they related to each other as a couple and as Christians, some areas of their relationship needed realignment.

Debra found talking to Mary much easier than talking to Dr. Fry. She felt a rapport and a bond only able to be experienced between women. When Jerry closed the door to Mary's office after their interview he asked, "Maybe you would like to set up a schedule of appointments with one or both of these doctors that we have seen today. Dr. Fry is right when he suggests that starting therapy can only benefit our case." They sat down in the outer office of the center to further discuss the idea.

"I feel so much more at ease with Mary than I do with Jonathan. Marcia has indicated that the trial won't be for another couple of months," Debra said looking for an excuse to stuff all this again, "so we have lots of time to decide, don't we? I've agreed to see Dr. Fry but do I have to also see Mary at the same time? I don't want to go into therapy at all but if that's what I have to do to win my freedom then so be it. I just don't see any reason to jump into anything more right now."

"Deb, talking to anyone can only help you. I know you hate to think of all this, that you would rather put your troubles behind you and pretend that none of this happened but it did and we have to deal with it. The court won't let you hide your head in the sand this time. If you feel more comfortable with Mary than with Jonathan Fry then why not ask her receptionist to set up your first appointment here instead of at Clarkville. Check with Marcia to see if the court will recognize this center as they would the psychiatric facility. We'll also find out if Jonathan will still testify even if you don't choose to go to him for therapy right now."

Victoria, the receptionist, overheard this last statement of Jerry's and interjected. "Sorry to interrupt you but I couldn't help but overhear your last remark. We are recognized by the courts and our therapists have testified on numerous occasions."

"Terrific!" said Jerry, "Then, Deb, if you want to talk to Mary, let's get this appointment made so we can head home. On the other hand, I have a great idea. Why not leave the kids with my mother and then we can have that quiet evening we've been wanting for so long. No kids? Does that sound wonderful or what?" Jerry was all playful trying to get Deb's mind off her need for therapy. They both had always believed in working out their own problems themselves, especially Jerry, but this time they appeared to need outside help.

Dragging her feet, Debra asked Victoria to set up another appointment to see Mary and as they discussed the cost of each appointment, Debra once again hesitated. "I don't see how we can afford all this, Jerry. We'll have to mortgage our house, as it is, to cover the cost of this trial. Where are we going to come up with money for therapy too?"

"Honey, I don't know but maybe the church can help out. I've heard that there's a plan that can help with this kind of therapy." They hadn't attended their church in the weeks since the incident but they knew that they needed to get back there. "In the meantime, don't worry about the cost. We'll manage somehow. Let me handle that hurdle, okay."

"All right, I'll come in on the thirteenth. Could I come in first thing in the morning? That way Jerry can drop me on his way to work and I'll only have to take the bus one way. This stupid driving restriction is hard to take but I guess I have no choice but to get used to the bus again after all these years." Debra resented her loss of independence.

"The morning would be fine." Victoria marked the appointment in and waived good-bye as the Wiebe's left for their home. They felt so good as they left Mary's office. At least they knew there was someone who could help them. Differently than Dr. Fry, Mary was treating them as a couple although she would see Debra on her own in the beginning. They were in better spirits than they had been in days and their decision to allow the children to stay with the elder Mrs. Wiebe had them anticipating a cozy evening for two.

When they approached their house they knew something was wrong before they even pulled into their driveway. There were a lot of people standing on the sidewalk in front and they were pointing to the front door. Jerry told Debra to remain in the car so he could check out the situation but she couldn't sit still. She followed him up the front walk amidst pointing fingers and loud whispers. When they arrived at their front door, they saw a message spray painted across the entire door. Both ran towards the back door, locking it after them. Then they called the police.

Debra was crying hysterically now and Jerry was so angry he knew he would hit someone if any of his neighbors said anything to them. How could anyone do something like this to them? They had always been good neighbors and had helped several of them out over the last years of living in this neighborhood. This was so unfair.

'MURDERER' and 'DEATH TO THE MURDERER' were messages neither of them expected to see on their front door. Those words, however, were in plain sight for the entire neighborhood to witness. When the police arrived and started asking questions of the neighbors, they discovered nothing. No one had seen anything or heard a sound and yet this had happened in the middle of the day.

The police said it was probably just some kids playing a prank because of all the publicity and that there was nothing they could do about it. They would keep an extra watch on the area and if they caught anyone, that person would be charged with malicious damage. In the meantime the Wiebes should keep their windows and doors locked at all times.

Debra made a quick phone call to Marcia. "They've got no right to harass me. Is there something we should be doing to avoid this or do we just sit here and take it?" she asked.

"Ignore the newspapers and the neighbors. It's just like the kid in the playground who's being hassled. As far as the newspapers go, there's not much more they can do now anyway. They'll just keep trying this case in their papers and the prosecution won't be able to select an unbiased jury in this state, that's all."

"With Jonathan's testimony, we will be able to plead 'not guilty' by reason of temporary insanity and since he's considered an expert witness, your case will be provable. Your sentence and your place of confinement, if you are held, will then be up to the judge to decide. Since you are not now insane, that will work in your favor."

"Do you mean that I may not have to serve any time in prison?" Debra was astonished.

"No, not if we can prove that you are not now insane but were at the time of the crime. In other words you need to keep your nose clean and follow the judge's orders to the letter. No driving…and keep a lid on that anger of yours. With the testimony of both the officer who saw you commit the crime and Jonathan, it should be easy to prove that you were insane but are not now."

Marcia was confident that she could prove her case but she was concerned about public opinion damaging her client's confidence. "Try to forget what went on this afternoon and we'll hope that the furor in the papers will die down."

"Marcia, would it hurt my chances if I decided to go to the counseling center instead of through Dr. Fry for therapy? I feel so much more comfortable with Mary but I don't want to jeopardize my chances with the courts either."

"I don't think it will make a difference since both agencies are recognized by the courts. However, it sure wouldn't hurt you to see both and will only prove more strongly to the judge that you intend to get to the bottom of this."

"I'll think about that. Thank you for all your help, Marcia. I don't know what we would have done without you." Jerry and Debra both were grateful for her help.

"I'm only doing what I get paid for and we still haven't won your case yet. Let's just pray that all turns out as we hope." Marcia was reluctant to think too positively yet. She didn't want to become overconfident. "I'll talk to the both of you again in a day or two. In the meantime, carry on as best you can in your normal fashion. Bye for now."

"Good-bye Marcia and thanks." Debra was already thinking about dinner and she wanted everything to be perfect. She and Jerry had not had a whole evening to themselves for a long time. They were going to enjoy it in spite of the writing on the front door. In the meantime, Jerry was searching for some fresh paint to cover the obscenity, so they could forget there were people out there who wanted his wife dead.

By the time the paint on the front door was repaired, Debra had thrown together a quick meal for the two of them. They ate sitting on the floor in front of the coffee table with some slow music on the stereo. Reluctant to turn on the TV after all the damaging news reports they had heard lately, the Wiebes continued to talk about their future and their family. They also did something they had not done together in a long time. They read their Bibles and prayed together.

Before long it was time to pick up the kids. Jerry left the washing up for Debra to do and he drove the short distance to his mother's home. The kids were ready for him when he arrived so once again a hasty good-bye left the elder Mrs. Wiebe standing on the doorstep alone. She always enjoyed having her grandchildren over but their exuberance made her tired too. She had gotten used to the peace and quiet of living alone since her husband had passed away. The kids seemed to enjoy being there and that felt good. Mrs. Wiebe wished that her son and his family were happier, though, and although she and Debra had not always agreed on things, she knew that the woman was incapable of killing anyone. Things would be better when they could all put this behind them.

Jerry and the children arrived home to a quiet, tidy home with soft music still playing on the stereo. They said a hurried hello to their mom and immediately went upstairs, a habit they were developing that their parents planned to break them of when this was all over.

"Matthew, Cindy..." Debra called them back downstairs. "There's something we need to tell you." Earlier Jerry and Debra had decided to tell their children about the paint on the door. If this could happen right on their doorstep, the kids were probably experiencing some harassment at school.

Debra began as soon as their two youngest were sitting in the living room. "How could someone do such a mean and hateful thing to us," sobbed Cindy. Her tender heart was broken for her mother's shame and agony at discovering that someone wanted her dead.

"The world is made up of all kinds of people. They only know what they read in the newspaper," explained Debra. She put her arms around her distraught daughter just as Matthew stated, "I'll find out who did this and punch their lights out," His protest was declared in all his adolescent manliness. "They aren't going to hurt you, Mom, and get away with it."

"We just want you kids to be safe," added Debra, "but thanks for standing by me, you guys. I know that this hasn't been easy for either of you. How are the kids treating you at school?"

"Oh-h-h, well" began Cindy.

"We're just fine," Matthew quickly interrupted thinking that his mother did not need to worry about anything else.

"Well if you ever need anyone to talk to, I'm here. I will be starting some therapy next week to help me control my temper better so things are going to be different around here from now on." Jerry stood by while his wife declared her intentions and watched as the children looked on skeptically. They had heard such promises before from their mother but it was never long before she blew again.

"Your mother's right," he assured them not for the first time either. "I will be taking her to her appointments before work every time and we plan to get this house back the way it was. We really do appreciate you sticking by us though."

"Of course, we'll stand by you and Mom," exclaimed Cindy. "After all you have stood by us when we messed up...Oh sorry, I didn't mean that."

"Never mind," Debra quickly set her mind at ease. "Tonight, your dad and I had some time alone to talk over some things we've needed to discuss in a long time. It felt like a date," she said with a twinkle in her eye. Matthew could remember when Debra and Jerry used to go out together all the time. That was before his brothers had become so wild, though. They hadn't relaxed much since the two of them had left the house either.

"We just needed to be by ourselves for a little while," explained Debra, hugging her two youngest. "It's late. Why don't we all head to bed. We can talk more tomorrow."

"Deb, why don't you take a long leisurely soak in the tub while I lock up," suggested Jerry.

"Ohhh…that sounds heavenly." Debra followed her children upstairs, turned on the hot water in the bathtub located in the room adjoining their bedroom. She added some fragrant bath gel and stepped into the warmth just as the phone rang on the bedside table. Drying her foot off and wrapping a towel around her, she answered on the fourth ring.

A voice, not recognizable, spoke harshly into the receiver. "Die, you murderer. I hope they throw the book at you. You murdered in cold blood and they will prove it." The person hung up with a slam of the receiver and Debra stood in shock. Just as she was about to faint, Jerry walked into the room. He caught her as she fell and gently lay her on the bed.

"What happened? I heard the phone so I came up to see who it was. What did they say to you? Deb, are you all right? Talk to me." Jerry was getting scared. Slowly, she opened her eyes and stared into his with tears bubbling over the lower rims.

"It was a man. He said 'Die, murderer, die, and then he said, 'I hope they throw the book at you.' He said some other things too. Oh, Jerry, I was so scared. Why are people doing this to us and who could that have been?" Debra's now chilled body was shaking and her teeth were chattering with a nervousness she had never experienced before.

Jerry thundered to the phone and placed a call to the police lieutenant who had been there earlier that day. "I want you to catch whoever is terrorizing my wife," he said. "This is probably the same person who painted our house. I want him stopped." Jerry was furious and wanted to protect his home but didn't know how. He was so frustrated and the police seemed to be of little use.

They held out no hope that they would be able to trace the call and the lieutenant seemed to think this could be an isolated incident anyway. "Besides, Mr. Wiebe, you could just not answer your phone the next time and the perpetrator will give up."

"Thanks for nothing," Jerry shouted and slammed down the phone in the lieutenant's ear. "They are never here when you need them to be and yet when you don't want to see them, they're on your back like leeches." Debra had never seen him that furious and she cringed away from him.

"OH, honey, I'm sorry. You've been through enough without me ranting and raving. Are you all right now? Go get in the tub and the next time the phone rings, I'll answer it, okay."

The rest of their evening was colored by the constant ringing of the telephone. When they answered it, the person on the other end would hang up. Finally about eleven o'clock they took it off the hook after phoning Jerry's mother to warn her she would not be able to call them.

Jerry snuggled down into the warm bed beside his wife and she quickly moved over to place her head on his shoulder. He placed his arm protectively around her and it didn't take long before they were both sound asleep. Tomorrow was another day and one that brought them closer to some real answers, they hoped.

CHAPTER SIXTEEN

Another two days went by without further incident. The family decided Sunday would be a good time to get back into the swing of things at church since it had now been close to a month since they had attended. They believed that their church family would welcome them back, showing them all the love, and support that they had always exhibited when the Wiebes or anyone else needed it.

Their preparations the night before was similar to that of a big celebration. The kids were excited to be going back and Jerry and Debra felt that they had a large hole in their lives without the fellowship of other believers. The entire household went to bed extra early in anticipation and were out the door the next morning at least fifteen minutes earlier than usual.

When they entered the foyer, they were not sure what to expect but knew that at other times everyone had rallied around when they needed them. This time was different however. They soon felt ostracized. No one came up to them to talk as they had in the past. Instead people stared and talked behind veiled eyes and turned backs. The Wiebes felt judged, misunderstood and above all disappointed, that the family of believers they had associated with for ten years, were so callous and uncaring.

Undeterred, they remained hoping that their brothers and sisters in Christ would accept Debra's repentance and they would be welcomed back. That never happened. The family was forced to admit that they needed to seek another church, one that didn't know who they were, as if that could happen.

The rest of their life had taken on a semblance of normalcy. The strategy for Debra's trial was all planned. Marcia had a full list of people to interview and prepare subpoenas for, starting with the mechanic who had taken Debra's car apart bit by bit. In two days, Debra's second appointment with Mary at the counseling center was scheduled.

The fall colors were out in all their glory. The Wiebe's had canned and frozen everything they could get their hands on to save money and by Tuesday, they had found a local bible study group from a church they were thinking of going to, nearby. Their life had actually settled down into a routine again and the tensions usually evident were almost non-existent. The children were enjoying a full schedule at school and sports activities became their focal point.

However, as Debra entered Mary's office the next morning, she felt the weight of not being as put together as she would have liked to be. She couldn't be normal if she had killed someone. Jerry didn't deserve a wife who was not whole and she was determined to fix whatever it was in her personality that made her so explosive. Mary was a quiet, calm, gentle example of someone walking with the Lord.

As the session progressed, Debra began to talk about her children and all that had happened over the last four years. Mary asked frequently how she felt about certain things but Debra had trouble expressing her feelings. She really didn't know how to put words to what she felt, she discovered. She was able to describe how she felt as if there was another part of her, a second Debra whom she was keeping out of sight. She had felt for a long time that if others knew that other person, they would not like her.

Mary was able, in that first session, to help her see that somehow she was keeping her feelings under so tight a control that she felt as if she had another person inside. It was as if she kept that part of her hidden so she could not get hurt again and yet pain was something she felt so easy.

Time sped by quickly after that. With counseling sessions every week and sometimes twice or three times a week, Debra was no closer to discovering what had her so tied in knots. She was beginning to think that her time and money was wasted at the center.

Christmas was approaching and the kids were involved in the youth group activities at church as well as a part of the community theater production of Nutcracker. Cindy was doing well in school but Matthew's grades were slipping. Every time Marcia came over the children would hide in their bedrooms and hardly ever acknowledge that she was in the same house.

For two months now, Mary and Debra spent their time together talking about Debra's life before and after her Christian conversion. They talked about her parents but Debra never bothered to complain too vehemently. She seemed to talk about her life as a robot with a detached sense of herself.

In the meantime, they were also exploring how her inability to control her temper had affected her marriage.

Mary assured Debra that she was not the only one that needed fixing. Jerry's personality was such that he allowed a lot of what happened. His need to be respected and in control was undermined daily. Debra's need to be in control was evident as they explored her fears and anxieties.

About a week after the two-month anniversary of Debra's first official session at the counseling center, the Wiebes were once again at their bible study enjoying the companionship of these new friends of theirs. The group had already become rather cohesive and this night they celebrated someone's birthday. All night Debra had experienced heaviness in her spirit and during their prayer time, she couldn't keep her tears at bay. Towards the end of the evening, she slipped away to the bathroom but then when her emotions became overwhelming, she quietly secluded herself on the back landing of their friend's house so as not to alert anyone of her distress. She couldn't understand what was happening to her but she hurt deeply.

She crouched in the corner, aware that somehow she felt a physical pain that had been inflicted years ago. No one was hitting her but she felt the welts on her legs as if a large, soap encrusted razor strap had flailed her as in her childhood. The sobs, she tried to garner some control over, were loud to her ears and she was sure their friends would all come running at any moment. They would wonder if she was having a breakdown and she wouldn't be able to say she wasn't.

Her emotional pain was so real but she didn't fully understand the cause for the physical pain. She knew her emotional pain was from a long time ago. Mary, her therapist, had explained that she needed to take out that pain and feel, as she had not allowed herself to do in her past. Maybe it was like getting "Chicken Pox" or "Measles" as an adult. The physical complications were more severe as a grownup person but she was so confused and she hurt so deeply.

Deep, deep into her very being, wherever that was, she could feel sorrow. A sorrow so clear that she knew it was real. Imagination could never feel like this, could it? Could she have imagined all the abuse from her childhood, an idea her brother accused her of when championing their father? He said she had deserved everything that Dad had done to her but in this incident, the one she was feeling so strongly now, she was only three years old. What could she have possibly done to deserve this amount of pain? It was no wonder she shut down her emotions then. It was so painful even now. How could a three-year-old have handled it?

The worse part was the knowledge that he hated her. Her father, whom she looked up to, whom she felt was her protector against the nighttime fears, hated her. His face had contorted so that she really didn't recognize him as the same face she loved to meet at the door each day after work.

When he raised the belt, he had seemed to put his whole strength behind it and the searing, burning pain of each blow seemed to indent her bottom and the back of her legs till they would never be the same again. Her screams made him angrier so she stopped. She held her breath and shut her eyes so tight that she was sure she was not there and that someone else was the one being beaten.

He had left her then with her bare bottom exposed as she lay on the bed sobbing deep but as silently as she could in case he came back. She fell asleep like that and dreamed that he came to her and hugged her and said he was sorry. But he never did. He never hugged her even when she was "good" so why would she think he would do it when she had been so bad. And it was her fault.

Daddy would never treat her like this if she didn't deserve it. When she awoke, she slid her legs to the edge of the bed, and on her tummy so she wouldn't hurt her bottom anymore, she crawled off the bed. That bed always seemed so big and it was so high up, but as her feet hit the floor, she pulled up her panties gently so the welts wouldn't be touched, and went out to say she was sorry.

As these memories flooded her mind, she sobbed again for that little girl who lost so much that day as she, for the first time, admitted that what had happened to her as a child was indeed abuse. Oh the child development specialist had called it that but she had never really believed it. Until now. She had lost, at that young age any illusion of a father's love, tenderness, and protection. Most important of all, she lost trust. He seemed to love her little brother but for her he had always been harsh.

As she crouched there, contemplating the little three year old that she was so long ago, she realized he didn't love her. Even now as an adult, she found that hard to understand and so painful to acknowledge. What was there about her that was so unlovable, that the man whom Mom had said wanted a little girl so much, could come to hate her? She had learned many things that day too and these lessons would repeat themselves various times over the years. She learned that to express one's emotions brought more pain so she could shorten the punishment by not crying out loud.

She had never quite mastered not crying at all but she could be quiet and if she turned her head away from him, he would never know she was crying at all. He never did notice her heaving shoulders it seemed, or maybe he just didn't care.

Footsteps were approaching and Jerry was beside her. He took her in his arms and held her, asking what was wrong. Debra couldn't explain fully, just that she hurt and she was only three years old. Mary had told him that she would experience something from her childhood, so he just held her and his arms tried to block out the pain of her youth.

More people were coming, and her friend encouraged her to come into the kitchen as everyone else from the study had left. She hugged her and it felt so strange. She was used to her husband's touch but she had never allowed too many people to come this close in the past and a hug from another adult made her stiffen. They did their best to comfort her but she was almost locked into that world of the past and her deep searing hurt blocked their attempts to soothe the hurt away.

Jerry and Debra went home but she continued to feel so strange. Was this for real or was she really just a loony after all? Panic rose to the surface but she decided to hold on till she could talk to Mary tomorrow. Mary would know what to do and would help her to understand. Her eyes were so puffy. Her husband had only ever seen her cry like this twice before in their whole married life and those times she had been so angry.

There was no anger this time, only the pain. Maybe all she was feeling was self-pity. God seemed to be saying to her that she was to allow the feelings and get to know them. It was then she realized God was there. Right in the room with her and in fact touching her and comforting her. He wanted this to happen and His Holy Spirit seemed to be directing her memories. She slept then but the heaviness stayed with her throughout the next day. Mary finally returned her call around 4 p.m. and after the counselor explained a "flashback", confidence in her own sanity returned.

"A flashback is the body's attempt to right what was made wrong so long ago," she said. "When they come just let them and feel everything that you never allowed yourself to feel all those years ago. What your father did to you was abuse and you have been a tightly contained person ever since, afraid of your own emotions."

It took a few days for the depression to subside but Debra did heal, or maybe "heal" was not the right word for it. She only knew that she felt somehow different and until she saw Mary again, she would just have to be aware and confident that the Holy Spirit was doing a work in her.

CHAPTER SEVENTEEN

Her next visit with Mary was different than the previous ones. She knew now for a certainty that she had been abused as a child and that until she dealt with it, all the denial in the world was not going to help. She had heard all the stories about forgetting the past and getting on with your life but now knew it didn't work, at least not for her.

She cried easily these days and discovered that it was all right to shed tears. Her two selves had integrated so she knew she was different on the outside, too. Jerry began to notice a softening in her personality and so did the others around her. She became more sensitive to others and learned all about walls and people bumping into them.

Those walls of protection she had used to shield herself from involvement in other peoples lives had also shielded her from their involvement in her life. She also knew that God and the Holy Spirit were telling her to learn to feel again and to allow others in her Christian community to help. She learned that in order to cope with the pain she experienced in childhood, she had locked away her feelings and every time she was threatened in any way, she added another row of bricks to the already towering wall around her emotions.

This wall caused others to bounce off her as she exuded rejection. She didn't trust anyone but especially men. As young as three years old, she had learned they couldn't be trusted. She didn't know how to feel as a 'normal' person would but she was determined to right the wrong thinking imbedded in her psyche.

The next time her memories flooded over her, she let them, choosing not to fight the pain but experience it. She remembered a time when she was about five years old.

At five, she still slept in a crib but it was a large, iron one; the type, she supposed, that was most common in those days. She had been awakened by some shouting and knew that her father had finally come home and even though she was only a small girl, she knew he was drunk again.

The bedroom Debra shared with her brothers and sisters was right next door to her parents. She could hear him when he blamed her mother for his foray into drink that night. She hated the shouting and then...her mother was crying. She only wanted to close her eyes and go back to sleep so she wouldn't know what was happening to her family. He got drunk very seldom but when he did he was so angry and could be violent. They all knew to keep their distance at those times.

Her father had other ideas though, and before Debra could cover herself fully, he was there. By this time her brother was awake but her father came beside her crib first. She stood as tall as his shoulders, standing in that crib, and felt so good that he was coming in to see her. She felt proud that her father was talking to her as a grownup, too, but when his words penetrated her mind, she was so frightened.

He told her that he was going away and wouldn't be back. His slurred words didn't cover the fact that he was angry, very angry. He wanted her to decide which of her parents she wanted to live with. In her youthful mind, she reasoned the cause of their anger to be her. After all, he never seemed to like her.

He never did anything with her, never hugged her or touched her except in anger. Maybe if she chose him, he would love her. Of course, she could never hurt her mother like that and although her mother seemed to be a quiet parent, she knew that a separation would hurt

pleaded with her daddy to stay and to love t

again. She started to cry, but he slapped her hard and told her to act her age.

He hated her tears and they always made him angrier so she choked them back but continued to plead for an end to this talk of leaving. "We need you, Daddy," she sobbed. She didn't know any other words to convince him to stay but knew she must anyhow. He asked Debra repeatedly to make the choice but she couldn't. All the things he said, about the fun they would have, she closed her mind to, for she knew nothing would be any fun if her parents weren't living together.

After a while he became so tired, he just fell on the davenport that was in their room and she could hear his loud snores not long afterwards. As she lay in the dark, she couldn't understand why their mother didn't come in to check on them. Her mother never interfered when their father was with them.

Looking back, these many years later, she couldn't remember what transpired the next morning but her mother used to let her father just sleep it off most of the time. Her memories flooded her like a wave of deep sorrow, so deep that her very soul was part of the pain. She remembered things long forgotten and with the remembering came the feelings that should have been expressed at that time long ago. As painful as the memories were, Debra now knew why she behaved as she did.

Suppressed emotions were hard to relearn so many years later but she would undo all the repression her father had instilled in her. Then she would teach her children all that they had missed by having a parent so closed up. She hadn't abused them, as do so many survivors of abuse. At least she hadn't in the usual sense. Somehow though they felt the lack of a mother who knew how to share her feelings with them. This missing piece of their life had hurt them almost as much as beatings would have.

They didn't share feelings either, and one of the complaints they'd always had about their parents, was that they couldn't talk to them. Jerry especially, but both of them, had tried to draw their children out but had somehow failed miserably. They had never been able to understand why their oldest two could hurt them so much, feeling no regret. Now Debra understood that children need to be modeled feelings as well as behavior.

One afternoon, shortly before the trial was to start, Marcia appeared at the Wiebes doorstep with a grin on her face. Her usual lawyer somberness was gone as she excitedly explained a new development in the case that had just come to her attention.

"This explains why everything you felt was so exaggerated and you committed a crime that normally you wouldn't have ever done," Marcia exclaimed. "When we explain this to the jury they will have no choice but to find you not guilty. The matter of your abuse is still evident but coupled with this new disclosure our case is stronger than ever. I hope this good news for a change will help."

"Thanks, Marcia, it does. I knew that there had to be something to explain all of this and somehow I was not too confident in just the abuse theory although I already can see how badly damaged my thinking was. I can't wait to tell Jerry. He'll be so relieved."

Now Jerry and Debra excitedly awaited the trial and as the date grew closer, Debra became more and more involved in her therapy. Even though she knew they couldn't afford the extra expense, she knew she was receiving the benefit, as was her whole family. She didn't jump down people's throats or overreact quite as often as she had in the past but she found that her emotions were still very raw.

With all the pain she was remembering from childhood, she had little composure left for her trial. All the worries that event caused only added to her raw emotional state but Mary and Dr. Fry, after several visits with him as well, both felt her emotional state could only benefit her case. Jonathan explained it would help the jurors to understand how childhood trauma could affect a person the way it had manifested itself in Debra's case.

The day of the trial dawned clear and very cold. Winter was almost over but the vestiges of the long struggle into spring remained. Maybe they should have had a dry run, Jerry thought, as they ascended the steps to the courthouse. He was nervous and he could only imagine how Debra felt.

She had been sleeping better and thankfully, their two offspring who worried them so much had been on their best behavior for a long time now, it seemed. The doors to the courthouse were really heavy and told of an era of tradition as they opened onto a long, dark, marble hallway. A set of elevators at the end took them to another equally long hallway, which led directly to the courtroom they were seeking.

Debra clutched Jerry's arm and her eyes were the largest they had ever been. Inside she was terrified and her head remained bowed as she tried to avoid the stares from the spectators who would sit through her trial. They paused at the door to the courtroom as Jerry reminded her she had nothing to fear and she needed to hold her head up as Marcia had instructed. She was not a murderer and she needn't feel or act as one.

Debra looked around her on the walk up that aisle toward the table she would share with her attorney. People actually sneered at her or was that, too, something she imagined. Her guilt, in the past, had made her see things that weren't there but she felt that this time her assumptions were correct. People believed that she was guilty of a far greater crime than what she was accused of. Debra hoped they would change their mind as they heard the evidence.

She was almost sure she was having an out-of-body experience as she went through the motions of sitting and standing at the appropriate times that day. This was all so new to her and so unlike watching television. These lawyers used different terminology than the ones on television. Marcia needed to explain a great deal of the proceedings to her client but things started very smoothly anyhow.

Opening arguments progressed in the usual manner and then it was the Prosecuting Attorney's turn to begin to convince the jury, which had been selected the week before, of Debra Wiebe's crime of premeditated murder.

They began by calling the eyewitnesses to the crime. "Your honor," began the prosecuting attorney. "I'd like to call Mr. Jim Johnson to the stand." As Mr. Johnson smartly approached the front of the courtroom, he glanced at Debra. With a look of apology on his face, he moved into the witness box and sat while the bailiff swore him in.

"Mr. Johnson, can you tell us where you were on September 21, last year, at approximately 10 a.m.?"

"Yes sir, I can. I was standing waiting for the Lions and Dunn Street bus by the bus shack at 21st and Norman."

"Exactly what happened that morning that was out of the ordinary?"

"Well, my wife didn't get out of bed to make me any breakfast before I left and..."

"No, no, I mean while you were waiting for the bus."

"Oh, well, we was just standin there, another couple of people and I, when this car jumps the curb and heads towards the young man over by the brick wall beside the bus shack. The car hit him hard and then backed up and hit him again. You could hear his bones crunch and blood spurted everywhere. You could even see parts of his body split apart, the car hit so hard."

"Do you see the driver of that car in this courtroom?" the prosecutor asked a now trembling witness.

"Ye-e-s-s, I do. That's her, right over there," he said pointing his finger at Debra with that same look of sorrow and apology but with the added emotion the memory of that day caused.

"The witness has identified, Mrs. Debra Wiebe, as the person driving that car," the prosecutor stated the obvious. "That will be all Mr. Johnson. Your witness," he added as he turned to Marcia.

"Mr. Johnson," she began. "Do you know for sure that Mrs. Wiebe deliberately ran her car into the young man or could she have been experiencing some car trouble?"

"No, I don't know anything for sure. But who would do a thing like that on purpose in broad daylight with witnesses close by? Maybe her car might have been the problem. But the newspapers say otherwise, don't they?"

"I request that the last statement be stricken from the record, your honor," Marcia hastily interrupted the witness before he could put another nail in Debra's defense.

"The jury will disregard that last statement," he ordered the twelve people who would decide Debra's fate.

"I am finished with this witness, your honor," added Marcia as she returned to her place beside her client.

"You may step down," the judge said to Mr. Johnson and then to the prosecuting attorney, "You may call your next witness."

The prosecutor called the other waiting bus line passenger who corroborated Mr. Johnson's testimony and who also thought, on cross examine from Marcia, that it was probably mechanical failure that made Debra do what she did. Then the prosecutor called in Detective Sloan.

His testimony was damaging as he described the extent of the injuries suffered by the victim. He also told how the car had been inspected at the impound yard before Ms. Dixon retrieved it, and that nothing in the way of a mechanical failure was discovered. "In fact, while the car was quite old it was in fairly new condition with low mileage," he added. "It appeared to have been well looked after."

"Object, your honor, the witness is not a mechanic nor does he know the history of this car," Marcia jumped in.

"Objection sustained."

"Detective Sloan, from your investigation, can you determine whether Mrs. Wiebe deliberately drove her car into that young man?"

"Oh, that she did," Sloan looked with foreboding towards Debra. "There were no skid marks, no indication that the brakes had been applied and she hit him with such speed that it appeared she never attempted to slow or turn away from him. Oh, she did it alright."

"Thank you, Detective Sloan. Your witness."

"How many 'accidents' of this nature have you investigated during your lengthy career as a police officer?" asked Marcia. She knew that he had only been assigned the homicide division the week before Debra's accident.

"This is the only murder of this nature," he replied.

"I object to his use of Murder, when it has not yet been proven, your honor," Marcia pleaded.

"The jury will disregard that last statement. You may rephrase, Detective," he directed.

"This is the only incident of this sort that I have been involved with. There is that okay, Ms. Dixon," he asked sarcastically.

"Your remarks will be directed to the question and nothing else, detective," the judge commanded. "Another remark like that and I will hold you in contempt."

"Detective Sloan," Marcia continued, "Have you or any of your police officers found any link between Mrs. Wiebe and the victim?"

"She killed him, didn't she?"

"I mean, have they discovered a relationship between the defendant and the victim?"

"No, they haven't yet but we'll keep looking."

"You have had over six months. Don't you think you have had long enough?"

"We'll keep looking until we find it."

"In the meantime, your honor, I ask the court to consider a dismissal since the prosecutor has not been able to find the link that would prove premeditation."

"I will see both counsels in my chambers, right now," the judge looked stormily at his two colleagues in the courtroom. "This trial is recessed until tomorrow morning at 10 a.m."

"All right you two, why haven't you settled this before the trial began. Counselor you knew that the police had not been able to link the defendant with the victim. Why did you continue to enter a charge of second degree murder?"

"We were sure we could, your honor and it may turn up yet."

"You have had plenty of time. The charges are reduced to manslaughter and counselor, you had better be able to prove your case. Ms. Dixon, you knew before this trial started that the prosecution had not found their link. Why didn't you ask for a dismissal when they insisted on charging her with murder at the onset?" The judge was angrier than either counsel had seen him in a long time. The possibility of a mistrial was a very real issue if Marcia decided to follow that course after her defendant was found guilty, if she was found guilty, he thought.

"We'll reconvene in the morning and I want you both to get your acts together," he added.

The next day dawned bright, sunny and with plenty of birds to remind the people caught up in this trial that summer was just around the corner. Everyone was seated until the judge walked through his antechamber door and then the observers as well as the players rose to their feet.

"You may be seated," the bailiff ordered.

"Ms. Dixon, your request for dismissal is denied. Mr. Prosecutor, do you have anything to say in that regard?" He looked pointedly at the prosecutor's table.

"Yes, your honor, in light of the fact that we have not found a link between defendant and victim, we are reducing our charges to manslaughter." The hum in the courtroom rose a decibel or two and a gasp of angry protest erupted from the mouths of the victim's family. But no one spoke out loud in fear of being extricated from the courtroom for the duration of the trial.

"Proceed," the judge ordered.

"Your honor, I ask Dr. Philbin to come to the stand."

Dr. Philbin was a psychiatrist, hired by the prosecutor to examine Debra a couple of week's prior in light of the fact that Marcia was pursuing the child abuse angle. However, to Debra he appeared not a very sympathetic doctor to the survivors of child abuse and in fact accused them of feeling sorry for themselves and trying to excuse bad behavior.

He did a lot of damage to Debra's defense even though he only visited with her once. All of this was very hard for Debra to listen to and still not allow her feelings of guilt to overwhelm her. Her self-esteem, she knew, was poor and the testimony of so many who thought she was guilty, hurt her a lot.

"Dr. Philbin," Marcia began her cross-examination. "How many victims of child abuse have you encountered, counseled and helped on the road to recovery?"

"As I said, I don't believe in long term effects of child abuse so I have no record of having helped any of these so-called victims."

"So, just what makes you an expert of child abuse?"

"I encourage people to get on with their lives and that would be my counsel for your client if she were to see me. I help people move forward, not backward!"

"That'll be all. You may step down," the judge ordered after Marcia indicated she was through with this man. "You may call your next witness."

"We rest our case, your honor," stated the prosecutor and now it was Marcia's turn. Once she started her defense of Debra, it was much easier for her client to sit through. Debra hadn't realized how much work Marcia had gone to until she listened to some of the testimony from people she thought had forgotten all about her. Marcia had found old and new friends and these people cared about her. They even testified of her accomplishments and she thought no one credited her with any brains at all.

CHAPTER EIGHTEEN

The most informative, from the viewpoint of expert witness, was Jonathan Fry. He commended her for having the courage to face her 'demons' from the past, as he called them; although she would have preferred he call them memories. He told the jury and those present in the courtroom that the mind was like a trap, holding hostage any emotions and memories that a person had during the course of a lifetime. If a trauma were not dealt with, he explained, most likely the mind would trap those feelings until such time as they could be expressed. Another part of his testimony was to relate one of her memories from about the age of twelve. She had shared this with him only the week before during one of her sessions with him.

When she'd had this flashback, it had occurred in the middle of a service at the family's new church. The overwhelming feelings had just about destroyed her composure completely that day so when she went for a visit at Clarkville with Dr. Fry, she had disclosed what had occurred. She'd wanted to hide from all the rest of the congregation but they'd sat so near the front that she couldn't escape. With the help of one of their new church friends, she had been able to get through the church meeting that followed the service as well. She hurt to the very core of her being when she asked, "Why couldn't he have just loved me?" Her father's love would have solved so many of her problems in later life.

Like all her other memories, it wasn't that she hadn't remembered at all. It was just that the emotions came with the memory this time and the pain was incredible. This flashback was about a time when she should have been excited about life wondering what wonderful things were in store for her.

She'd been fast approaching puberty and her mother had handed her a booklet sometime during that year describing changes that would occur in her body. As she had read it she had felt very grown up. She was also embarrassed, though, and there was no way she could discuss it with her Mom.

Besides according to the stories she'd heard at school, she supposed she was lucky to have been told at all. She kept the knowledge to herself feeling very much a woman when 'it' happened a week later. Several weeks after that, she had been visiting in the home of her 14-year-old cousin, when her cousin asked Debra to join her in the bathroom. With a look of terror and a question of whether she would die, her cousin pointed to the toilet. She knew nothing of what was happening to her, so the twelve-year-old educated the 14-year-old and felt very adult.

It was an early age to have already started her monthly cycle but she had also started wearing a training bra. Her mother and her aunt liked to tease her about that though so she stayed out of their way as much as she could. She had lots of friends but had already learned that life was unpredictable.

Not too many months before, on another visit to her cousins, a young girl she used to play with died when the house she lived in caught fire. Before the firemen could get to her screaming form in the upstairs window, the house had collapsed around her as the neighborhood residents and visitors watched in horror. Her memories of her friend never left her and every time she passed the spot where the house had stood, she felt the same horror.

Debra would quickly think of something else, though, and for the most part her life was all right. Her father hadn't beaten her in a few years now so she hoped that part of her life was better. He still didn't talk to her too much except to tell her to do things or not to do things. In fact her memory of those days with her parents was dim.

Until the day her parents came home and told the family that their father had been diagnosed with an addiction to codeine. They explained that some codeine was in the pills that Dad took all the time for his chronic back pain and that he would have to go into a private hospital for a while to get rid of this habit.

In those days, drug addictions were not common, so she never thought too much about it. He was sent to the hospital and her mother used to visit with regularity. Debra remembers visiting once and it seemed like such a nice place to be. Each bedroom was decorated in pretty wallpaper with matching bedspreads and curtains. The room her father was in, was yellow and seemed so cheerful when compared to her own bedroom at home and by this time he seemed to be very cheerful too. Could the pills have been the cause of all the bad times in the past? She wondered.

Six weeks later he came home and the twelve-year-old took on the role of the parent when her mother was at work. The medication they gave him to substitute for the codeine caused him to act very child-like. She had to keep a close eye on her father lest he go outside in his pajamas. He was so happy though and laughed a lot and she quickly grew to like this new side of him. She also found she could get away with scolding him when he was bad, and he didn't get angry.

Toward the end of this time, her mother and father went out to a dance one evening with an aunt and uncle. Her father had been told that on this medication, he was not to drink but that evening he had two beers. Another aunt had stayed with Debra but she couldn't remember her brothers and sisters being there.

When her parents returned about midnight, Debra was sleepily watching a good movie on the couch with her aunt, a privilege she didn't enjoy very often. She did not hear her father approach from behind her and when he pulled her hair and asked why she was still up, she did as she had done for weeks by then. She shoved his hand away and said," Leave me alone".

Her next memory was of running for her life. He was chasing after her shouting that he was going to kill her. She ran from him as fast as she could. She ran up the stairs and hid under the bed but he found her and so she quickly scurried out the other side. The bed was a double one, shared with two of her sisters and was too wide for him to reach her. She ran down the stairs again and pleaded with her mother for help.

By this time her pajamas were very wet but she couldn't remember having soiled them herself. She couldn't remember having been this frightened before either, and the butcher knife he was brandishing meant that he was serious. She also couldn't remember her father moving this fast before.

Her heart was beating so hard she felt like it was going to come out of her chest. Many thoughts went through her head during this interminable time when she was sure she was going to die. That he hated her this much seemed so unreal but her terror was the real thing. Debra remembered thinking that if he hated her this much maybe she should just stop and let him kill her. After all she was mad at him too and thought she would like him to go to jail for murder.

251

Finally her mother stepped in her father's path but to no avail. He simply pushed her aside against a chair and chased Debra once again up the stairs. She knew now that there was no one to help her but when she dived under the bed again, he just stopped chasing her and went back downstairs. Later she discovered the reason.

When he had pushed her mother against the chair, two of her ribs had been broken and he had to take her to the hospital to be looked after. While they were gone, she cleaned herself up; very embarrassed by the mess she had caused. By the time her parents returned she pretended she was asleep.

The next day her father was very sorry for what he had done to her mother but he never apologized to Debra. He served his wife meals in bed and told her that he loved her. He said he would never drink again but the family knew that it was only a matter of time.

Debra avoided him as much as she could. She had a hard time looking him in the eye, and she knew she would not trust him for a long time, if ever. She hoped her brothers and sisters didn't tell the kids in the neighborhood. She didn't want anyone to know her father didn't love her and that she wasn't worthy of their friendship. Her father never mentioned the incident to her, and she never even expected an apology. He never had apologized in the past, and she knew, he never would.

As Jonathan Fry read this recollection, the courtroom was silent. Many of them could relate to similar incidences in their own lives. Debra's pain was felt by all. Jonathan explained that children react differently in similar circumstances but that in this case, Debra had been traumatized to a point where she actually buried deeply any feelings she may have had at the time.

"Her feelings of fear, pain, and above all, the realization that her father wanted her dead, were all forgotten as she survived the only way she could. She discovered that her feelings could be used against her so she denied ever having those feelings."

"Would a person, having experienced this type of trauma at such an age, react with memory loss when experiencing another trauma so much later in life?" Marcia asked.

"She certainly would. Memory loss can be another survival technique used to deal with the intense feelings she was experiencing at the time."

"Thank you doctor. There are no further questions. You may cross examine."

"No questions for this witness your honor." The prosecuting attorney looked bothered by this testimony but trusted that the jury would remember the gruesome crime committed above all else.

Marcia continued, "Your honor I'd like to call Officer Jacobs to the stand." The gasp was audible from the courtroom, as everyone knew he was the police officer who had witnessed the incident.

After he was sworn in, Officer Jacobs was asked to state his name and occupation. Once stated, he then went into detail about what he saw. The prosecutor was smiling. They knew this testimony could be very damaging to the defense but he also knew that Jacobs intended to tell the jury that Marcia was not coherent. He had been excluded as a prosecution witness for that reason.

"What was the defendant's state of mind when you stopped beside the car?" Marcia asked.

"She seemed out of it. By that I mean, she seemed not to know what she had done or where she was."

"Objection, your Honor," piped in the prosecuting attorney. "The witness is testifying to a fact when that fact hasn't been proven."

"Objection sustained."

"Officer Jacobs, what did you observe from your point of view?" Marcia tried another approach.

"She acted the same as many people I've picked up on drug related charges. She was looking around to get her bearings and when I approached the car, I frightened her as if she had been jumped at from a dark corner. She really seemed not to know how she had ended up on that sidewalk and she certainly didn't seem to know what she had done."

"Did she act guilty in any way?"

"No, only confused and distrustful. As if we were lying about her."

As Debra listened to the various testimonies, her mind drifted to her last flashback. She had fought this one for two days but after listening to herself yell at the kids for no reason, bite her husband's head off over nothing, she finally submitted to the pain stored for so many years. Actually, Jerry forced the issue one night, pushing her to experience the emotions and to focus on how long ago that was.

This time he also experienced the pain with her and knew she would be better for taking this memory out, dusting it off and making friends with her life. These memories made her the woman she was today, he thought, and the person I fell in love with.

CHAPTER NINETEEN

Fifteen had not been such a bad year. In fact, as scared as Debra was when they moved to the big city, it hadn't taken her long to make some good friends. Now, of course, she knew that her parents were not rich since some of the kids attending her high school were children of ambassadors and high-up government officials. They were the 'in' crowd at school and she knew right off that her father would never let her be one of them.

He had set the rule as soon as they had moved that she was to come home right after school and since this 'in' crowd met at a local soda shop at that time of day, she was not invited. Of course, there were other reasons she wasn't asked to join them. Her clothes were hand-me-downs and looked it. Nothing ever matched and even if she had known how to match them, they had a worn look. All of the other clubs met after school as well so she was relegated to only her academic studies.

At school, she came to know three other girls quite well and they hung out together in between classes. They were older than she was because she had been placed in the 11th

grade when they moved, and should have been a sophomore. In her last school, her marks averaged over 80% but in this big school, with its three-foot thick walls and 10 classes of each grade, she quickly became lost.

The distractions were many and since her parents had never discussed college with her, she knew she was headed for the working world right after graduation. Her friends also never talked of college so the foursome would dream of their jobs after high school and helping out at home with room and board. All she wanted to do was to be able to buy new clothes that were all hers and to be asked out on a date.

She had the usual complaints, she guessed, about her parents, for up until that time she never really thought they were different from other parents. Another friend, who lived just down the street, was an only child. They would go together to the neighborhood hangout once in a while but her parents never let her go to many places after dark.

For some reason, unbeknownst to her, Debra's father and mother decided to join the local "United Methodist Church". It had not been a priority before so she really was not interested and the few times they could talk her into going, she found nothing to hold her there. The sermons were dry and usually about the same things as the evening news. She couldn't remember them ever using the Bible for more than a reading each Sunday. Her time there was usually spent checking out the hats or someone's beard.

One Sunday, at the beginning of summer, she was really tired and did not want to get all dressed up, so she convinced her parents to let her stay home. After they left, she tried to go back to sleep but she was too wide awake so she got up, got dressed in a pair of shorts and went down the street to her friend's house.

Lorraine lived next door to twin boys who were about 21 years of age. Before long the girls were talking to the boys from Lorraine's front porch. Peter and Paul were good looking and they seemed to like Debra too, or at least Peter did. Paul was already going steady with someone else.

She was enjoying herself so much she lost track of the time and the next thing she knew, her brother was standing on the sidewalk, telling her that her dad was really angry and she was to come straight home. "Boy, you're really going to get 'it' now," he said. She figured if she were already going to get 'it', she would impress the boys by *seeming to be her own boss. She sent her brother home with a message that she didn't believe him and continued to laugh and flirt.*

It didn't take her long to discover she had made a big mistake. Within a few minutes, her father was coming to get her, carrying in his hand the cord from their electric iron. These removable cords were like coils of wire wrapped in a woven fabric and were stiff. She didn't know whether to run or continue to joke it off, but she had nowhere else to go.

Lorraine looked on in horror, having never experienced a beating in her life, as Debra's father whipped her the first time across the back of the legs and then again and again as they walked quickly up the street to their home. The pain was excruciating and welts appeared immediately. Varied emotions, from embarrassment at being treated this way in public to sorrow that he still could not ever love her, turned to defeat when she realized this was just the beginning of her punishment.

The look on her father's face told her he was very angry and he always took a long time to cool off and then only after she had been thoroughly beaten. He whipped that cord back and forth across her legs all the way up the street to her house and up the stairs to her bedroom, where he proceeded to finish the job. She tried hard not to cry but the pain was worse than anything she had ever felt before.

The tears ran silently down her cheeks. He'd make sure she wouldn't be able to wear shorts all summer, he'd said as he called her a whore and a bitch in heat. She was used to those names since they seemed to be the common ones he used to describe her since she had become a teenager and discovered boys. Debra's mother was nowhere in sight but Debra really never expected her to be. She had no one to defend her and she had no where to flee.

After a while, he stopped but not before he had covered her legs in welts. The physical pain was awful but worse than that was her realization that other parents did not treat their kids this way. Watching Lorraine's parents, who called their daughter "Love" and put their arms around her, Debra longed for just that kind of caring. Some of the boys made fun of her at school so maybe she deserved this treatment but she began to think she was just unlovable.

The next morning, when she very carefully rolled out of bed, she was appalled at the bruises covering her and ashamed to be seen that way. As hot as it was, she wore dark stockings to school. Slacks were not allowed in those days. She had to watch how she sat in the desks each class so her bruises wouldn't hurt more.

No one asked her about the way she was dressed so she got through the day, keeping her terrible secret to herself. As if it had never happened, everyone at home carried on as usual. All she wanted to do was curl up and die but she felt they wouldn't have cared anyway. There was no salve for the welts, no pat on the back to let her know someone cared and no alliance with her siblings. They seemed to enjoy her pain and she knew it would never be any different.

Out of defiance, the little streak of rebellion that she had left, she wore her shorts in the house, to let them see what he had done to her. There were no comments. It was as if she were invisible and their life just carried on the same.

One of those times, Lorraine came to call. Much to Debra's horror her mother let her friend in and although she tried to hide the damage, it was all too visible in her shorts. Shame washed over her but knowing Debra really well, Lorraine said nothing until they were at the door and out of hearing distance of everyone else.

"Do you want my parents to call the police?" Lorraine asked. "What he did to you is called abuse." Debra didn't think the police would do anything so she told Lorraine 'no' but the comfort she felt from those few words was heartfelt. Someone really cared about her. She buried it inside herself to warm her for the long days of loneliness ahead.

Abruptly, she was brought back to the present as Marcia called her next witness. "Your Honor, at this time, I'd like to call Buddy Smith to the stand." Debra knew this was the moment they had all waited for. This was when they would prove their case once and for all and then they would be finished with all this stuff and get their lives back to normal. The Judge chose that moment to look at his watch and since it was nearing four o'clock, he felt that the court could be recessed for the day.

"Also," he explained, "since the court is occupied for the next two weeks with another matter and the Easter break is scheduled, we'll reconvene this case after the holidays."

Darn, Debra thought, just when we were so close. She was saddened at the Judge's lack of compassion for her and what this delay would cost her but as she silently sent up a prayer to her Lord for patience, she looked at Jerry and noticed a glint in his eye, not seen for so many weeks. Curiosity distracted her and she smiled back as she tried to imagine what her inventive husband had up his sleeve.

CHAPTER TWENTY

Jerry was ready for her questions when Debra walked out of courtroom but he wouldn't disclose anything to his curious wife. She continued to badger him all the way home but he was very evasive in any answers he did give her. "I wonder what he's up to," she thought to herself as they pulled into their driveway.

Jerry, a romantic when he put his mind to it, had arranged for a weekend surprise. Debra was just going to have to wait until later to find out what it was. Since it was Friday, as soon as they entered the house, Jerry grabbed the already packed suitcases and threw them into the back seat of their car. Debra really had her curiosity aroused now but he held fast to his secret.

She and Marcia had dropped the kids at her mother's place when Marcia had picked them up for her court appearance that morning. Unbeknownst to her, Jerry had arranged for them to spend the entire weekend. Her mother lived on a farm, a place that the kids always enjoyed and were forever asking if they could stay over.

The children were looking forward to a weekend of fun with Grandma and Grandpa and the opportunity to work in the barn with the new calves. Debra's mother had remarried just after Jerry and Debra had tied the knot and her husband was a nice man. Farm chores had been neglected over the last few weeks in support of Debra so lending the older couple the willing hands of their grandchildren was one way the Wiebe's could repay their support.

Jerry and Debra had always spent a weekend once a year, away by themselves, just to keep the spark alive in their marriage. This time Jerry knew they needed the time more than ever so had planned somewhere special. Once Debra knew they were headed for some time alone, she relaxed and her smile returned with all the warmth Jerry knew she was capable of.

Not more than two hours away from their home was a resort designed for married couples with luxury cabins each containing it's own hot tub. When they arrived, Debra looked around her, enjoying the early signs of spring and the fresh scent of the ice melting on the lake. Jerry quickly parked the car and ran around to her side to open the door for her. He leaned into the interior and very slowly kissed her with a tenderness only he was capable of.

The Wiebe's didn't think about who might be watching them as the years and fears melted away and their passion caught fire. The feeling of coming home was always there for Debra any time that Jerry kissed her. She emerged from the car tingling and a warm flush crept up her neck when she looked into the face of the resort manager, grinning from ear to ear at them. Jerry scrambled to check in and then they were on their way for some much needed privacy.

Their cabin was everything Jerry had hoped for and as Debra saw the hot tub, a giggle of anticipation erupted from her throat. This hot tub was more the size of a small pool. Although not big enough for one to do laps in, it was large enough for some romantic fun time. They both looked at each other with cloudy, seductive, bedroom eyes when they saw it.

Their bed was a waterbed, once again designed for romance with drapes surrounding three sides and a large control panel on the headboard. This they assumed was a stereo but they couldn't wait to see what else this cabin had in store for them. Since it was still seasonally cool, the fireplace was lit when they arrived so the warm glow that greeted them relaxed them on the spot.

Hot hors d'oeuvres awaited them as they unpacked hurriedly. Once seated before the fire, they unwound slowly nibbling the prepared treats and washing them down with mulled cider. Once the dampness and cold was removed from their bodies they felt really relaxed and with awe watched, an hour after they arrived, as a waiter brought them a meal fit for a king right to their cabin door.

Jerry had ordered all of Debra's favorite foods including a large salad with French dressing, steak teriyaki, baked potato, and plenty of vegetables. He even ordered her favorite desert whispering that she deserved every delicious bite. The waiter discreetly set everything on the table including a couple of candles, which he lit before leaving the two to their romantic interlude.

They ate with relish wondering when the last time was they had felt this carefree. "At this resort," Jerry told Debra, "Meals can be served in our room or we can indulge in some fantastic items off the menu in the restaurant, which provides the best cuisine for miles around. How do you like things so far?"

"Oh, Jerry. You have no idea how much this means to me. I love all this and you know I'm a sucker for the romantic routine."

"Let's just enjoy every minute while we're here and forget all that we. er...you've been through this past year, okay?" Jerry wanted to get to the place they had once been in their relationship. He was glad Debra was responding and he was so proud of the progress she had made at the counseling center. He knew it wasn't an easy thing for her to go through but he was happy she was and proceeded to tell her as much.

"I want to be the kind of wife that you deserve," she answered, "and I plan to work hard to get there one day." Debra was feeling the warmth from the good food and the relaxing atmosphere. "Let's try out that hot tub, shall we," she flirted as she began to slowly unbutton her blouse. She headed over towards that area of the cabin with Jerry not far behind and the evening began to take on a life of its own.

Over the next two days, the Wiebe's experienced every thing the resort had to offer. By the time they were packed to head home, they felt like two lovesick newlyweds. They knew their relationship had been cemented once more but they also knew that without their eyes constantly on their Lord, they would stumble again. Jerry was amazed at his wife's composure these days, as there were fewer and fewer things that seemed to bother her now.

She laughed more and teased him all the time. She actually flirted with him all the way back to the city and she hadn't done that in years. She had grown so much closer to God too and could worship him openly as never before. He knew she was much stronger since her sessions at the center had begun. The financial hardship was still there but the rewards were too great to stop them.

When they turned down their street, they passed the local high school and once again Debra's thought processes brought her back to a time when she was in high school. Jerry knew instantly that something had changed when she became so very quiet and her tears started to flow. When he stopped the car in the driveway, he pulled her into his arms and held her as she related this latest of her painful memories.

He wished with all his heart that he could punch her Dad in the face for all this pain he had caused her, but the man was dead so he just had to deal with his anger another way. Maybe he would have to see a counselor for his own peace of mind for he knew that he was hearing things from Debra he had no way of handling emotionally. All the stories fostered such anger in him. All he could do for now was listen and try to understand.

High School, a time in everyone's life when lifelong memories are created, was to Debra a memory to be forgotten. For a long time she never thought of those days for they held no pleasant memories for her. They were years of fighting with her father, sneered at by her siblings, and dreaming of better times ahead.

Graduation meant nothing to her since she knew she wouldn't be going to the prom anyway. Her hand-me-down wardrobe didn't lend itself to prom attire and besides no one from her school had ever asked her out. Not being allowed to participate in any of the after school clubs, she only got to really know the same four girls since she had begun attending this school. She felt awkward, shy, too flat, too tall, and mousy with no sense of style all through her high school years so all she wanted to do was get over them and get a job.

A full time job represented her escape, a chance to be an adult. She wanted her parent's respect and she wanted them to love her. She felt that if she could contribute financially to her upkeep, they would love her more. For the previous six months, she had worked at a butcher shop after school, on Friday nights and all day Saturday. She received a total of nine dollars each weekend and that money was handed over to her unemployed boyfriend for their once a week date, a date she wouldn't have had if she had not been able to provide some money.

That money wasn't enough though so the end of school meant more hours to earn more money. By the age of sixteen, she had finished high school and with the recommendation of her boss at the butcher store, she obtained full time employment at a bank as a teller. She was so excited. They liked her work, although she was the youngest in the branch and they all acted like her parents looking out for her all the time. She really enjoyed the work. She was learning a lot and when she received her first paycheck, she thought she had struck gold.

Debra had never had so much money all of her own before, money that she had earned herself and she felt very proud of her accomplishments. It had never even occurred to her to discuss the decision to work full time with her parents. She looked upon it as a natural progression from one stage in her life to another.

The bus trip home that day was so long. She wanted to tell her parents what she had accomplished and watch them smile with approval. As she sat looking out the window, she imagined the look of support on their faces as she handed them her room and board.

Although they had never discussed it, she was sure they would accept half of her paycheck every two weeks but she was willing to give them more if they wanted it. As long as she had enough for some new clothes, she didn't need any more. Her heart was beating very fast by the time she got home but she went about doing her usual chores. She couldn't wait till her parents got home.

They were both tired when they walked in the door so she put off telling them until they were at the dinner table. As she related how she had gotten the job (they still thought she was working at the butcher shop), their faces changed and she wasn't sure why. She handed her mom the money and all her father asked was "What about college?"

273

College!! That was the first time she had heard those words come from either of her parents mouths. She had always assumed they were too poor to send her and so she had never mentioned it. Now she heard her father saying they wanted her to go back to school in the fall. That was the man who had argued against everything she had ever learned in high school. He denied the existence of dinosaurs, he argued against the history she was learning, or anything else that she tried to share with them about her days.

Now he wanted her to endure more of the same for an education that she had never even thought about. When she remained adamant about the bank, instead of approval, she heard her father say, "You have 24 hours to get out of this house. I don't want to see your face when I get home tomorrow night."

24 hours! Just one day to find a place to live and she knew he meant it. She also knew that she would be gone permanently this time. This would be no weekend stay at her cousin's like when she was in senior high and her father had told her to get out. Those times he never said anything when she came home on Sunday night for school on

Monday but he had also never said he didn't want to see her face anymore, either.

She left the supper table devastated but with a strong look on her face. She would not let them see how hurt she was and she had learned long ago that the only opinion he listened to, was his own. Going up the stairs to the room she shared with her younger sister, she wanted to cry but tears had never helped before. They had in fact made matters worse so she swallowed a lot instead. She started taking things out of her drawers and the closet, folding them to put in bags for the trip to her new residence, wherever that would be.

Getting up that next morning for work was really hard, since sleep had eluded her the night before. She had still not figured out what she was going to do but she had to go to work and maybe there she would find a place to live. Her salary was only $105.00 every two weeks so she did not have a lot of money to spend on rent somewhere. There was no such thing as welfare in those days or people who slept on the streets either; at least not from the world she knew.

She waited until she heard the front door slam, signifying her fathers departure for work, before she went

275

down for breakfast. There, she half expected to hear her mother say her father had changed his mind. In contrast she found out that she was not to call or visit and that her father didn't want to hear her name mentioned. Her mother was hurting, she could see, but she had never known how to stand up to her husband.

Instead she arranged a time to see Debra once a week at a location downtown across from the bank in order to touch base with her daughter but she wouldn't tell Debra's father. It was a long sleepy ride to work that day full of sadness and resolve not to let it show.

The first offer of a place to stay came quickly and she was relieved. The day passed and after work she quickly went home and just as quickly left her parents home for the last time. She knew she would not see her father again or this house and the pain inside was like a large hole in her soul. She stoically acted as if this was all perfectly normal.

Moving into the tiny bed sitting room was not so different in many ways than the bedroom she'd had at her parent's house but it was different in other ways. A bedroom was all that comprised her whole house or living quarters now. Also her new roommate informed her she would be alone every night until the wee hours of the morning. She didn't explain what she did after her work hours at the bank, just that she wouldn't be home after work each day.

It only took three days to find out what extra curricular activities replaced her roommate's daytime job. One evening the phone rang; which was unusual. No one ever seemed to call her roommate and none of Debra's friends knew, yet, of her new living arrangements. The man on the other end of the phone asked for her roommate and when he was told she was not in, he asked if she wanted to take Marietta's place. Debra asked what for and was told in very explicit language the nature of his business with her friend.

Prostituting herself was the way her roommate could afford to live here and wear the kind of clothes she wore. She was shocked! What had she gotten into now? How was she going to get out of that mess?

However, the dilemma seemed to right itself when Debra shared what she had learned at work the next day. She was careful not to embellish the conversation between herself and the man on the other end of the phone the night before, but her friends conclusion seemed to match hers. An older woman, Margo, was married to a man who served in the air force. Since he would be away for the summer, Margo thought she could use the extra help with her young son. Arrangements were made for Debra to move the next weekend.

*After work that night, Debra prepared to go out with her boyfriend. When she had moved from home to this small, shared room, he had seemed supportive. He still took her out when **she** could afford it so that evening was no different. They went for a long drive.*

It didn't take long for him to display a different side to his character, however. They ended up in the country not too far from where he lived with his parents. He had decided that since no one else cared for her, why should she care about remaining a virgin. While she knew his statement was correct to some extent, she still knew her mother would be disappointed, so she remained true to her convictions. Walking home was the price she paid for those convictions but her pride in herself grew a little too.

The next day, at work, plans were finalized for her move to Margo's on the weekend. Margo's husband Don had approved of the idea and would be there to help. Debra would have to share a room with their three year old but at least she would be protected and treated like a sister instead of a potential business partner.

Margo was like an older sister and Don, the big brother. They had an adorable little boy and Debra thought that finally life was going to settle down. She was almost 17 but she felt like an older woman of 25, at least.

Each week, she got together with her mother for lunch since her mother worked not too far from where the bank was. The week before her birthday, her mother invited Debra and two of her friends over for birthday cake. She timed it so that her husband would not be there and she baked her daughter's favorite cake, chocolate. When Debra arrived with her friends, they were the only ones there besides her mother.

She never asked where her brothers and sisters were but she assumed they weren't there so they wouldn't be able to tell their father Debra had been back. However, her father arrived home earlier than expected. As soon as he saw her, he told her to leave, she was not welcome there. Her friends were mortified and she was once again reminded that she was worthless in his eyes. Continually confronting his feelings for her was bad enough but with someone else to witness it, it made it more real. She left their home once again and it would be a year and a half before she saw or heard from him again.

"Why couldn't he just love me as other fathers loved their daughters, Jerry?" She sobbed and her heartbreak became his. He knew that he could console her by telling her that a lot of other people go through a worse childhood than she had but he knew that she needed to cry out all the pain hidden for so many years. Once she allowed her pain to catch up with her experiences, she could get on with her life accepting that that was just the way it was. For now she needed the hurt to sharpen her feelings and sensibilities.

Debra wiped her eyes and looked sheepishly around. The night had turned really cold and there were no neighbors to see her making a fool of herself in their driveway. She loved this man who had put up with so much from her over the years and she knew beyond a shadow of a doubt, this was why God had provided such a man for her.

"Do you think I'm being silly, crying over all this after all these years? Sometimes I think I'm just a big baby, feeling sorry for myself and yet the feelings are so overwhelming that I haven't a lot of choice how I react. When my memory is about some physical pain, I feel that pain as if it was all happening right now. I don't fully understand it but Mary said that this is all quite common. I'm sorry I ran my mascara all over your jacket."

"Honey, don't worry about my jacket. Besides I have this cute little housekeeper that does a great job on my clothes."

She punched him on the arm and they kissed. "Deb, I know this is hard on you but it's also hard on me. I want to hit anyone who could cause you so much pain, but you've become so much gentler and softer in a nice person sort of way. I wouldn't stop all this for anything since I see the person God intended you to be coming to the surface more and more every day. We'll continue to hang in there together."

"Oh, Jerry! I love you so much. You are just what I need when these moods strike and with your help, they are becoming easier to overcome all the time. Already, I feel better, although I probably will still need a couple days to get my spirits 'up' again. Let's go in and call the folks to let them know you are coming to get the kids. I have another appointment with Mary tomorrow and I'll be able to talk all this over with her."

CHAPTER TWENTY-ONE

Easter was a busy affair, as usual, only this year Debra enjoyed the holiday more than at any other time. Jerry's family knew little of this process of surviving child abuse but seemed to want to forget her criminal charges for this day, anyway. She felt closer to her Lord than she had ever in her life. Celebrating His sacrifice was more meaningful than ever.

If nothing else ever got better as the result of her therapy, she would be grateful for the closeness she was experiencing in worship. Ever since she started to get in touch with her feelings, became integrated actually, she had been able to love the Lord with a completeness never before experienced. She knelt at His feet regularly, if not in actual fact then figuratively, and the depth of the love she felt for Him overwhelmed her. Where once her control of self had been her focal point, her submission to the Lord's will for her became the most peaceful experience she had ever had. Also she had expected to be incarcerated by this time but instead the courts were still not finished with her case.

The Tuesday right after Easter, the whole family, at least the adult members, was in court again and although Debra was not as frightened as that first day, she still felt intimidated by the stares and the proceedings.

After the preliminaries, Marcia called the witness she had last called before the recess. Buddy Smith was the second mechanic responsible for assessing the damage to Debra's car and he, like the first one, had not found anything mechanically wrong with the car. As he was sworn in, the courtroom looked on with curiosity wondering about this witness and what he could possibly contribute to this trial.

"Mr. Smith, can you tell us your occupation and how you are connected with this case?" Marcia wanted to obliterate any doubts as to this man's credibility.

"I work for Lawson Mechanical Services as a licensed mechanic and was the only one not too busy to pick up Mrs. Wiebe's car a while back."

"Can you tell us in what capacity you continued to be involved?"

"I was hired by the Ms. Dixon, through the service station, to inspect the car."

"What did you discover in the course of this inspection?"

"I was cleaning out the back seat area and found a mat soaked with some smelly stuff. In fact, the odor from that mat was so strong, I had to put it somewhere else so I could work on the car. It gave me a headache, ya know. So I took the mat out and put it in a plastic bag so I could eventually return it to the Wiebe's. What they was gonna do with it, I don't know. It smelled that bad. Anyhow, the next day you showed up," he pointed to Marcia, "and you got real excited when I told you about it. You asked me to give it to you. Here's the receipt you gave me for it."

"Thank you Mr. Smith, no more questions." Marcia waited while the prosecution declined cross-examination and then proceeded to call her next witness.

"For my next witness, I'd like to call Dr. Winegartner."

An elderly man slightly bent over, walked through the thick doors of the courtroom. He was distinguished looking but not without the appearance of having worked hard over the years. A buzz had erupted from the spectators who wondered about this man's connection to the case so the Judge had to ask for quiet.

Once he was seated and sworn in, Marcia asked her first question. "Dr. Winegartner, can you tell us your occupation and where you are presently employed?"

"I'm a chemist employed by Waterburn Laboratories," he answered.

"What exactly do you do at the laboratory?" asked Marcia.

"I am currently working on the effects of certain chemicals on the human brain," Winegartner replied.

"When I brought you the mat, were you able to identify the chemical that had soaked into it?"

"Oh, yes, it's quite common. Androstadienone is a steroid found in sweat, auxiliary hair, blood and semen. It is a common ingredient used in the manufacture of perfumes and colognes."

"What effect, if any, does this chemical have on the brain of humans in a confined space such as a car?"

"Usually, this product is quite harmless when used in a small quantity as a perfume but a scan of the women's brains, in a study done recently, after exposure to this steroid in a closed environment and for more than ½ hour, showed increased activity in regions associated with smell as well as those areas associated with vision, attention and emotion. As in this case, it became a stimulant to the normal emotional workings of the brain. In other words, it has the effect of enhancing or exaggerating one's emotions."

"Can you tell us how it would work on someone who was angry to start with, an anger already identified as coming from child abuse, and someone who was very tired as well?"

"Well, her anger would be amplified to the point of 'out of control' and because she'd had little sleep the night before, it would affect what she remembered. She would be in a kind of euphoric state. This would manifest itself like a person on a strong drug but the effects wouldn't last as long."

"So that when Mrs. Wiebe opened her window at the bus stop after hitting the victim, she would appear to be lethargic and then confused, not remembering what had just transpired?"

"That's right, Ms. Dixon. The effects would wear of really fast and it would appear as if she were just waking up."

"Thank you, Dr. No more questions." Marcia was pleased with the testimony. By the hum reverberating throughout the courtroom, this new piece of evidence had obviously caught everyone by surprise and they were looking more sympathetically in Debra's direction. When asked to cross-examine, the prosecutor rose to his feet and proceeded.

"Dr. Winegartner, what is your experience with child abuse?" he asked.

"Why none except that most abuse suffered in childhood, I understand, manifests itself in extreme anger in adulthood. This emotion would have been enhanced by the chemical in the back seat."

"Are we supposed to believe that Mrs. Wiebe killed this man because of her suppressed anger and the chemical agent in the perfume?"

"Yes, that's right. My research has proven that emotions that are already out of control are stimulated further and the person has no knowledge of what went on during the chemical's involvement."

"No more questions, your honor." With that the prosecuting attorney returned to his seat. Marcia supposed he knew when his case was lost but she was not about to relax yet. Her summation lasted for over an hour as she detailed all that she had learned about abuse and the anger it produces.

"As people neglect to deal with their issues in an effort to forget their past and get on with their lives, they leave themselves open to more heartache as these feelings, long buried, surface," she said. "In conclusion, I will remind the jury of Debra's good reputation and the effects of chemicals in confined spaces."

Throughout all of this Debra's memories went for a walk again as she considered another time in her life. Her therapy had taken her over the most painful memories and she had progressed to the point of remembering but dealing with her pain as if it were a long ago event not a recent one. They were hurtful memories but a part of her now and events that made her the person she was today.

By the time she'd become an adult, she and her father reconciled. He had finally said he'd loved her but she believed it was just to get her come home. She'd moved a good distance away and developing a relationship by letter was difficult but she had tried. Her next visit home was to watch her father die after a lengthy illness.

The night he died, she looked around the hospital room afterwards, feeling confusion and another feeling that was strangely out of place here, indifference. Maybe it was the strength she needed to guide her through the next few days, but it didn't feel like a normal reaction to the death of a parent. Imparting the sad news to her brothers and sisters was very difficult. Her mother hadn't considered it her responsibility to prepare them in any way.

Her siblings viewed her as an intruder. After all, she had been kicked out of the home three years ago. Her father must have had a good reason and here she was telling them that their Dad was dead. She expected their hostility because they had lost any closeness that they once experienced as small children. Her brother had always treated her the same way as her dad had, with blame and intolerance. Debra was the cause of her father's anger when she was at home and now that she lived a long distance away, she had caused him to feel guilty, according to her brother anyway.

Following her mother's requests, she helped complete details for a long "wake", an eastern custom supposed to honor the dead. Debra wasn't even sure she liked Dad and yet for her mother's sake, she carried on as if she did. Her lack of tears puzzled her because no matter what he had done in the past, didn't everyone cry when their father died? It was like she was dead inside.

For three days, from 10 a.m. till 10 p.m., she sat with her mother beside his casket. She watched as people came to pay their respects and the tears that were shed seemed to mock her. "Really good people cry when someone dies" they seemed to say. And "See, it doesn't matter what he did to you. People still love him."

Her aunt, his sister, stalked up to her and in front of everyone accused her of being the cause of his death. No one defended her and she had long ago given up trying to tell others they were wrong about her. Even after her aunt had witnessed his attack on her with that butcher knife all those years ago, she could still defend him.

The funeral chapel was packed. So many were crying. What did it feel like to love someone that much and to be loved in return? If so many felt as they did, had God, wherever He was, made a mistake, when taking her father? There were men spending the rest of their lives in prison for serious crimes and all her father had ever done was beat her. She was of little importance, obviously; especially if you looked at all the people who thought he was so good. So, if there was a God, why did he allow her father to die and leave her mother to raise those teenagers alone?

After they lowered him into the ground, people went to her mother's house to console the family, she guessed. She didn't want to be with the crowd. They weren't there for her anyway so she went for a walk and sat under a tree in her black dress. She tried to think but she had no thoughts. She was just dead inside. Her eyes felt as if someone had packed them on the inside with cotton covered in a medicated ointment. She felt like everyone could see they were puffed out and the pressure was terrible. She felt so alone and so unloved.

There was no one in the world that really cared what she thought or what she felt. Oh, she was engaged by then and she used to think he would care but all he did was keep her around to satisfy his male ego. Whatever his needs were, she was there to satisfy him, but at least he wanted her around most of the time. For some strange reason, known only to God, she felt she didn't have a right to her feelings even then, so practiced her lifestyle of repression. Instead she worried about what she could do to make her mother's life easier. Never a thought of "Mother, would you hold me and comfort me, because I hurt, too".

Two weeks went by while she helped her mother sell their house. When the widow reminisced, Debra tried to be responsive. Her siblings were no help at all since they were in their selfish teenage years but she was only 19 herself. It seemed acceptable for them but not considered for her.

Tears were shed a few at a time by herself, hidden from her mother, lest that hurting lady break down again. She felt an overwhelming sense of responsibility toward her mother and she felt it was expected of her. Maybe she could change her mother's opinion of her or build anew the mother-love everyone talked about. When they removed her father's belongings from the closet, her mother asked her if she wanted an old ashtray set that had been given to her father. It had a chip out of one part of it but she accepted it anyway as a small memento. It would forever remind her of the Dad that found her too hard to love.

Debra sighed. As painful as her childhood had been, it was part of who she was and always would be. At least now she wasn't hiding from it and could accept why she was the way she was. The trust thing would come she supposed but at least now she knew why she reacted the way she did to men and could work around it, trying to trust and asking God to help her.

CHAPTER TWENTY-TWO

The trial was almost over. The prosecution had made a feeble attempt to present a summation worthy of the caliber of their expertise but the heart had been taken out of them when they realized the truth of the Wiebe's situation. They didn't want to send an innocent like this person to prison, not really, as long as she got all the treatment she needed.

It only took the jury two hours of deliberation before all of the parties involved were once again seated in the courtroom waiting for the verdict to be read. Debra's anxiety level was the highest it had been in her lifetime but her feelings were mixed with confidence, too. So many positive things had happened to her since all of this began and even though she would not trade that boy's life for those events, she was grateful to her Lord for bringing something good out of this tragedy.

What if they still thought she had deliberately run that poor boy down? Could she handle going to prison for a few years? She supposed that if God could bring her through the turmoil of the past months, then He could handle a couple of years.

Watching the faces of the jury, people who would be responsible for deciding her fate, she couldn't tell what they had decided. They must take some kind of course on how to be the perfect jury member or something, she thought. No city has that many stone faces. Then she giggled. What was she thinking about? Here she was, about to be sentenced to prison, maybe, and she was wondering about jury courses.

"Have you reached your verdict?" The jury foreman stood and handed their verdict to the bailiff as the judge asked the defendant to rise. Marcia stood with her and smiled confidently.

"We find the defendant not guilty, your honor." The foreman pronounced her freedom as if he had been someone's savior everyday of his life. Debra almost fainted with relief. Tears felt so good when they were from happiness and these days she no longer believed they were a sign of weakness.

"Mrs. Wiebe, I caution you," the Judge reiterated, "You need to keep up the good work in your therapy sessions and until the time when you are considered capable by Dr. Fry, you will not drive your car."

"Thank you, your Honor," Marcia replied. "My client would like to say something."

"Go ahead, Mrs. Wiebe, but be brief. It's been a long day." The judge was not so sure that the jury had decided a just verdict or that they were doing the defendant any favors.

"Your Honor, I would just like to say how sorry I am to the victim's family. If I had known that my past would produce such a rage, I would have dealt with it a long time ago. As far as the chemical, I promise not to carry an unsealed container in my car again. I don't know what I can do to show how sorry I am. Thank you."

Debra sat down again and the gavel signaled the end of a long nightmare as the Judge thanked the jury and dismissed them. Jerry rushed to his wife's side, as did both of their parents. Even Mrs. Wiebe, who was very undemonstrative, hugged everyone in the family. The press tried their best to get an interview but the Wiebes had already seen how the newspapers handled the truth when they tried her in the press before the trial and found her guilty without any regard to the facts in the case. The Wiebes chose not to see their statements distorted again so refused to make any statement.

Marcia however, held a press conference on the steps of the courthouse at which time she encouraged others, who were victims of child abuse, to seek help. "There are many victims of child abuse walking around today who are terrorizing their families and making life in general miserable for everyone around them because they have not seen fit to look after their past. They live under the mistaken idea that what's in the past can be forgotten. As Dr. Fry described during the trial, our minds are like a trap when it comes to anything that happened to us that was of a traumatic nature. Our minds do not forget and the memory will manifest itself in one way or another." With that said, she walked down the steps and got into her car.

Marcia was about to put her car in gear, when a hand rapped on the window. She turned to look into the smiling eyes of Jonathan and felt rather good that this time she had someone to share her victory with. She quickly rolled down the window and smiled her welcome.

"Would you care to have dinner with me tonight, Ms. Dixon?" Jonathan asked. "I figured you would be tired and in need of some company to celebrate. We could go to that restaurant we discovered last month and eat in that cozy curtained booth."

She blushed as she remembered the last time they had eaten at that place. Jonathan had virtually kidnapped her from her office late one afternoon. He had taken her to this very secluded restaurant where a pianist was providing the most romantic music. The maitre d' escorted them to a tiny booth, draped with curtains, away from the prying eyes of other diners. The meal began with a glass of rose-colored wine in fancy goblets with tiny crab cakes and shrimp as appetizers.

The evening had progressed from laughter, warm glances, and handholding across the table to a very seductive kiss at her door when Jonathan had insisted on driving her directly home.

Marcia, although very tired, was reluctant to refuse his invitation this time when he obviously thought it appropriate for tonight. They had been seeing each other as regularly as both of their busy schedules would allow for the last three months and the feelings manifesting themselves within the confines of Marcia's heart were getting stronger every day.

"I'm really tired tonight. Too tired to get all dressed up. Would you mind if we go to my place and just order in? Having you with me will be enough of a celebration," she pleaded. "I hope I didn't ruin some well-laid plans, Jonathan. Is it okay?"

"Honey, being with you is all I need too. Let's do it at your place?"

"Do what? Jonathan, what have you got up your sleeve?"

"You'll see. I'll follow in my car but let's get going okay," he said with an anxious glance behind him at the car he had left running on such a busy street.

She turned with the smile still in place and was greeted with sneers and lewd glances from several of the police who had been involved in this case. That didn't bother her though. She was too happy to let them get to her. The Wiebes had been so grateful for her defense of their family member and she felt really good that she could do such a good thing for such nice people.

Before they left the courtroom Debra had tried to express her gratitude towards Marcia and then said, "Come with us to celebrate. Jerry's taking us all out for dinner at the 'Captain's Table'. Dr. Fry is welcome, too." Debra felt a tinge of excitement and her heart was full of happiness. It had been a long time since anyone had seen her so carefree and she felt like she had dropped ten years off her life with the court's decision. All she really wanted to do now was to get on with their life and rest in her Lord for the duration.

Her older children were settling down, or so it seemed, and they were looking forward to a much deserved, but inexpensive holiday in July. The court's costs would take a long time to pay off but they wouldn't get too depressed over that today.

"I'm pretty tired and you really don't need to see any more of me right now," Marcia had answered and she was now glad she did. A time alone with Jonathan was just what the doctor ordered.

Debra had promised to call Marcia in a week or two for a lunch date and then the family had gathered for some more hugs of victory. It wasn't long though before she said to her best supporter, "Let's get out of here. I've seen enough of the inside of a courtroom to last the rest of my life." Jerry agreed and while he wanted to leave, everyone seemed too busy talking to hear what he said. Finally he managed to make himself heard over all the good wishes. "Why not continue this at the restaurant. Mom would you like to follow us in your car," he said to his mother, "or come with us and we can drop you back here later?"

"I'll meet the rest of you at the restaurant. That way I can leave whenever I want." Mrs. Wiebe liked to hang on to her independence.

"Mom," Debra spoke for the first time to her mother since the verdict had been read. "We'll see you and Dan there too, okay. Drive carefully." Debra gave her mom a hug before she started to move towards the door. Everyone else proceeded to follow. She was anxious to leave this place once and for all. Now that it was over, they could be a well-functioning family again.

Everyone waved and promised to meet in a few minutes as the traffic from the courtroom dispersed. The reporters were gone and the Wiebe's were looking forward to the time when everyone in the city would forget who they were, so they could get on with their lives.

Jerry quickly pulled his wife into an empty room by the elevators. He gathered her into his arms and for the first time since all this began, he cried. His sobs were almost loud in that empty room and for a second, Debra felt a little frightened. Jerry usually didn't cry or at least not like this.

"What's the matter, Honey?" she asked. "It's all over now."

"I am just so relieved that I'm not going to lose you, after all. The thought of you spending any time at all in prison has been torture and now that it's all over, the relief is so overpowering. Sorry I didn't mean to scare you, Deb."

"No, I'm the one who's sorry. I've been so wrapped up in myself that I've not given any thought to what you must be feeling. I'm so sorry I've brought such pain to you. Jerry I wish I were the kind of person you deserve."

"Honey, you are the kind of person I deserve and don't you forget it. God brought us together. There's no way we would have ever met if all those circumstances in your life hadn't played themselves out in the way they did. You are the person God chose for me and God cannot make mistakes. I just needed to release some of the tension that's been building. I'm fine now."

They hugged for a long time and didn't worry if their family would have to wait a little longer for them at the restaurant. They needed the strength they drew from each other and the comfort that only their other half, by God's standards, could give.

CHAPTER TWENTY-THREE
Epilogue

It had been two months since the trial had ended and everyone in the Wiebe household had settled into their individual routines again. Cindy and Matthew were studying for finals at school and the furor over their mother's trial had died down. The kids accepted that their mother couldn't help what had happened and even though there were still a few who chose to tease, most treated them as before.

Debra was still in treatment although she was only going once every two weeks now. Her talks with Mary at those times were so enlightening as she understood more of how she could compensate for her lack. She was beginning to understand that the trust she had lost would probably never come back. A small part of her would always distrust the people around her but she was trying hard not to let them know it. It was one thing not to trust but the kids and Jerry needed to feel they were trusted, especially the kids.

They were too young to fully understand the damage that had been done to her thinking but Jerry could and he compensated by making sure he didn't tease her as often in those areas where she needed reassurance. He knew that when he raised his voice, she would change instantly. It was as if a small fear would resurrect itself and yet he had never hit her nor had he ever threatened to. Before she had always reacted in anger when he got angry. Now, her softer self would almost flinch. The angry times were so far apart these days that they could almost forget how things used to be.

Jerry was back at the routine of his job. He never thought, before, that he would enjoy routine as much as he did now. He had had enough adventure or turmoil to last a lifetime and yet he knew that raising kids almost guaranteed some more. He hoped he had learned enough to be more sympathetic to someone else going through a trial in their life. He had also learned how much growing he needed to do in his faith and he hoped God would allow him to learn it naturally instead of in the fires of troubles.

They had seen Josh and Donald, their two oldest boys, frequently that first week after the trial but lately; they hadn't been able to get in touch again. Down deep, Debra and Jerry, separately, were apprehensive but chose not to voice their worries to each other. They didn't want their past experiences to color how they reacted to these two. They really wanted to get past all that and forget they had lost their trust in their two older children. It hurt too much to think of all the boys had done to their own lives unnecessarily.

Jerry knew, now, that the woman he had thought was so tough and confident was really very unsure of herself. He wanted to make her see, once and for all, her worth but all the years of being made to feel so worthless and from the eyes of the one man who mattered the most, next to him, had taken their toll. She was so beautiful to him and so special. She was learning to trust him as never before though and he believed and said often, that it didn't matter what had gone on in their life together, he loved her as she was. She almost believed him.

Just before dinner, on this warm May evening, the phone rang. Jerry had just arrived home so he quickly picked up the extension by his favorite chair.

"Hello," he answered. "Oh, hi Josh, where've you been? We've been trying all week to call you. Sure, we'll be home this evening. Yes, we'd like you to come by. See you then."

"What was that all about?" Debra asked worriedly. "They usually don't call just like that to come for a visit."

"Now, stop worrying, Deb. Maybe they're finally growing up and miss seeing us."

"Oh, wouldn't that be nice. Somehow I don't think that's the case though, do you?"

"Let's just wait and see, okay." Jerry was forever the optimist as far as his kids were concerned but Debra was acting as she had learned. No trust.

They proceeded with their meal and Debra put two plates of food in the oven knowing the boys had probably not eaten. Conversation around the table was animated as Matthew shared an incident that had happened at school. He was turning into the class clown these days. His sense of humor was really emerging and he seemed to really like and care for people. Cindy was becoming quite the grown-up little lady, whose love for the Lord over shadowed anything she did at home or at school. These two children seemed to have such a good self-concept compared to the two older ones and yet Debra and Jerry couldn't think what they had done so differently in raising them.

The dishes were quickly washed and put away and any homework was attended to. The television was airing a special about welfare fraud, which the Wiebe's had just started to watch, when the doorbell rang.

"Come on in, you two. I'll bet neither of you has eaten. I've got a plate of beef and macaroni casserole put aside for each of you if you want."

Oh, Mom that's all you ever think about...our eating. We're fine. Okay, okay. We'll eat." Their second son, Donald, wasn't one to turn down a free meal anyway. Josh, on the other hand, was always watching his weight. Debra worried about him becoming anorexic but he always told her not to worry.

Both children, for Jerry and Debra could never think of them as anything else, ate heartily, belying their protests. They were quieter than usual so separately Jerry and Debra began to suspect that, as in past, they wanted something.

"Mom and Dad," Josh began, "I need to tell you something. I know you've just come through a bad time but this won't wait. My girlfriend is pregnant and I want to know if you both will be grandparents to our baby. Megan and I want to get married but I need to go back to school to finish high school so I can get a good job. That'll take another two years since I've spent so much of the last couple of years playing hooky."

"I don't believe this." Debra was angry, yet calm, if that's possible. Everyone held his or her breath waiting for the explosion that would happen, as it always did. "Are the two of you planning on living together till then or what? You don't even have enough to feed yourself properly. I just don't understand how two kids who have been taught all the morals from the Bible can turn their back on everything we stand for. Oh, what's the use?"

She didn't explode! Everyone looked at her as if she would, though, so she had to stop asking questions and let it sink in. She didn't feel that sudden eruptive feeling anymore. It was gone. Oh, yes, she was worried about these two sons of hers who seemed so determined to wreck their lives. Now with their oldest bringing a baby into their world, she felt like a hole had been carved out of her insides without the use of anesthetic.

She didn't want to become a grandmother so soon but she would never advocate abortion. Her chest hurt with the weight of this latest dilemma.

"Mom, Megan and I love each other. We're not planning on living together. Donald needs a roommate so I'm going to move in with him. That way I can afford the rent and food too, okay. When school starts in the fall, I'll have to apply for student aid until the end of the first semester anyway. The baby is due in December and I want to stay home and look after it then. We just want to be able to bring the baby here for a visit from time to time without the roof caving in."

"You'll have to give your mother and I a chance to get used to this new situation," Jerry added. "We thought we had a few years to go before we would become grandparents. Have you considered all the angles? What about adoption? That way your baby could have a two-parent, stable home." Jerry hoped this would give his son a chance to grow up a little. He was only twenty years old. He was almost a baby himself and here he was going to have a baby. He never thought he could be so hurt. His girlfriend had been raised in a very unstable, single parent home too. What kind of mother would she be?

"Do any of you want anything to drink? We have some coke or ginger ale. Jerry we need to talk about something else for now and let all of this sink in." This was coming from Debra. She was calm. Her family looked at her and saw a strength they had never seen before. Jerry's eyes widened as he contemplated this new side to his wife. He started to grin.

"Okay, later Babe." He said and then winked at her for he knew she would vent with him later, then they would pray about this new crisis but then they would 'console each other' and boy!!! That was the fun part.

The rest of the evening progressed with calm. The family even pulled out a board game and the older two joined in for a change. The topic of the untimely pregnancy never entered their conversation again until Josh and Donald started to put their jackets on to leave.

Jerry was the first to speak and although neither he nor Debra had had a chance to talk, she agreed that they would support their son no matter what. He had a long hard road to travel with responsibilities beyond his years and, they thought, capabilities, but they would be helping any way they could without compromising their beliefs, of course.

Josh hugged his mother and father for the first time since he had decided he wanted no part of their God or their home. Maybe God would use this situation to bring Josh and Donald back to their roots, a foundation built on the love of Jesus Christ. With Him all things are possible, thought Debra confidently, as they closed the door and walked up the stairs to console each other and try out the title 'grandparent' on each other.

ABOUT THE AUTHOR

Barbara Ann Derksen began writing about fifteen years ago when her husband installed their first computer in the home. She has spent many hours since then perfecting this book but also working on several others. She began writing for local newspapers six years ago. Her first column, 'Help Me Rhonda', ran for a couple of months and then another newspaper picked up her column, 'Meet Your Neighbor', which has run in that and a couple of other newspapers ever since. Barbara has written over 1500 articles to date, which have all been published. Most of them are about the people who live nearby but she has also covered some news worthy events and local government meetings.

Barbara and her husband Henry make their home in Alta, Iowa. They have four children and six grandchildren. Besides writing, Barbara rides motorcycle with her husband for an organization called Christian Motorcyclists Association, is a certified scuba diver, and loves all species of animals. Their two dogs, Patches and Pokey, have spent hours at her feet while she completed this book.

Printed in the United States
17470LVS00004B/1-24